EERIE EXHIBITS

Five Macabre Museum Tales

VICTORIA WILLIAMSON

Silver Thistle Press

This edition published by Silver Thistle Press Ltd in 2025

Silver Thistle Press Ltd
272 Bath Street,
Glasgow
G2 4JR

For all enquiries, please email: enquiries@silverthistlepress.com
www.silverthistlepress.com

978-1-7384364-1-5

Printed in Great Britain

This book is dedicated with thanks to Glasgow Museums whose policy of making their wonderful exhibits free to public view has been an invaluable source of education and inspiration to me and many others growing up.

The Screaming Room

1.

When I was a child, I heard butterflies screaming. I was too young to understand the significance of that terrible sound back then, of course. But thirty years later, I discovered the cause of the Screaming Room's hellish symphony, and now I can never unhear or unsee those horrors.

It all started on a rainy day in August when I was eight. It was another bleak afternoon in an interminable summer holiday, with my father distant in more ways than one at yet another low-paid job, my mother heavily pregnant and moving with bovine torpor with my less-than-longed-for sibling, and my own small supply of childish creativity sapped by weeks of ennui. I was too quiet and sensitive a boy to make close friends, and the loose group of boys who suffered my presence in return for my submission to their regular cruel jokes were away sunning themselves in more exotic climes than my family could afford.

It was a surprise, therefore, when just after lunch, my mother suggested we spend a few hours at the Museum.

Given my family's financial constraints, day trips were

uncommon, but they'd become even rarer as my mother's belly ballooned and her steps became more ponderous. Needless to say, I already had my coat and shoes on and was waiting eagerly at the door with an umbrella by the time my mother had shuffled around our small kitchen in search of her handbag.

After so many weeks cooped up in our cramped flat, the bus ride through the rain-washed streets felt like the beginning of a thrilling adventure. The grey high-rises clustered around the traffic-clogged junction soon gave way to the grander sandstone tenements of the West End. Crossing the river, I pressed my face against the window, watching in awe as the swollen waters thundered beneath the bridge and gouged chunks of grass from the banks of the park. My mother's hands were gentle as she pulled me away from the greasy pane and wiped the condensation from my cheeks. She was smiling at me, then. I remember that, too. Despite her own discomfort, she still found pleasure in my enthusiasm for the outing, and her gaze was equal parts fond and amused.

I often try to conjure that look in my mind's eye now, on rainy days when the weight of memory becomes too much to bear. Sometimes I see it clearly still, while at other times, my recollections are overlaid with the ghastly scenes that came after, like a photograph that has been doubly exposed.

I digress. The bus trip to the Museum was, at least, an undiluted memory of pure pleasure and anticipation.

Back then, before the Museum modernised and sold off the bulk of its eclectic collection, the late Victorian-era building was a curious boy's playground. Its exhibits were loosely grouped into themes in much the same way that kitchen drawers full of odds and ends are loosely appointed as stationary holders or receptacles for various unrelated utensils. There was an equal chance of finding undiscovered treasures in the Museum's labyrinthine rooms as there was of finding long-lost yo-yos, stamps, foreign coins and yellowing photographs tucked under my mother's tea-towel collection.

We started in the Egyptian rooms, where I marvelled at the tiny blue shabti figures and shivered with excitement over the macabre stone sarcophagus taking up almost the full length of the passageway to the Roman exhibits. Passing along rows of marble statues and mosaic panels from classical antiquity in much the same desultory way I skipped over my carrots at dinner time, I soon led my mother to my favourite collection of all. Tucked rather eccentrically between glass cabinets containing stuffed animals, and reassembled dinosaur bones astride raised platforms, was the chamber of medieval horrors.

I was too young to fully appreciate the meaning of the iron maiden and the rack that took up one corner of the room, and my mother kept a firm grip of my hand lest my curiosity distract me from the portion of the exhibition she did permit me to examine. But her concern was unnecessary, as my focus was all on the gleaming suits of armour I remembered from my last visit, long ago. They were still there – the silver helmets and breastplates of knights poised for battle, the Italian suit richly engraved with gold and brass for some long-dead and evidently portly nobleman, and the giant model horse adorned with fitted plates over its flanks and eyes. I sighed with happiness, my imagination at last finding the food it craved after weeks stuck at home with little more than colouring books and cartoons to occupy me.

There were more delights to come – the Japanese chest with so many tiny drawers my head buzzed with the possibilities of what it might hold, the African masks whose sightless eyeholes followed me up to the first-floor gallery, and the apiary sandwiched between glass panels that opened onto a window where bees buzzed in and out, hard at work making honey despite the unseasonable weather.

By the time we'd wound our way around to the cabinets of fossils at the back of the gallery, my mother was panting and clutching her stomach.

"Jeremy, I need to sit down," she said, a pained look on her face. "Let's go and look at the paintings for a while."

I couldn't help feeling a sharp pang of resentment at my mother's constant tiredness. She'd always had the energy to run and play with me before. It had gone a long way towards making up for the contempt of the children at school, but now her gradual withdrawal from our games and the many hours she spent napping made me yearn all the more for the way things had been before 'the baby' colonised my mother's body and took her attention away from me. I hadn't asked for a sibling, and no one had consulted me about it. My parents had just announced it was coming and I'd soon have to share my little bedroom, and that was that.

I had something equally unpleasant to contemplate right then, though. The thought of sitting looking at endless scenes of painted sheep and bowls of fruit for even five minutes made me shudder with more horror than the understanding of the iron maiden's real purpose might have done. I looked around for an alternative. Anything would do, just as long as it wasn't boring old pictures in ridiculously ornate frames.

"Let's sit in here," I said, guiding my mother through an open doorway into a small room off the main gallery. It didn't look particularly promising, but there was a row of glass cases along one wall, and a flickering light suggested that a slide show of some sort was playing. It hinted there might be something more entertaining to look at than layers of dead paint, at any rate.

Glancing at the sign on the door as we passed into the room, I felt a shiver of unease tingle up my spine at the words I saw printed there.

'Screaming Room,' it said.

"Mother, what's a 'screaming room'?" I asked, tugging my mother's arm.

"What? Oh, a screening room is where they show things on film – you know, like a cinema," my mother said wearily, heading for the benches that were set up before a projector screen at the far end of the room. I looked back. She was right. The sign did indeed say, 'Screening Room'.

Smiling at my own mistake, I sat down beside her, eager to see what the pictures projected onto the wall were showing.

I was interested at first. The footage was of beautiful butterflies, their wings all the colours of the rainbow. I recognised some of the local species – Red Admirals, Cabbage Whites, Tortoiseshells and Peacocks. I'd seen them fluttering from the gardens of my richer classmates on my way to school, and my mother had told me their names. There were others, too, that I didn't recognise – their wings iridescent blue and vivid green.

But the film reel rewound to the start of its loop, and the butterflies were replaced with fat, ugly caterpillars which gobbled leaves and spun themselves into tangled cocoons. I got up in disgust. It reminded me too much of the way my mother had changed in reverse, her body swelling with the squirming creature that would soon be popping out and sucking her dry, while I would be left to my own devices and all but erased by the ravenous grub's all-consuming need.

My mother was already nodding sleepily, her head lolling on her shoulder. Her brown hair was tied up in a long plait, and in the projector's light, it shone radiant chestnut, a colour so temptingly rich I had to stuff my fists into my pockets to resist the temptation to run my fingers over it, in case I woke her up.

I wandered over to the glass cases against the far wall instead.

Inside were row after row of dead butterflies. I've mentioned previously that I was a sensitive boy at that age, but what I should perhaps explain, was that I had a particular horror of dead things. I'd once found a dead spider on the kitchen windowsill, its legs curled up beneath it, and cried for a week. When my father brought a heavy book down on a mouse that had somehow found its way up eight flights of stairs to our high-rise flat, I was inconsolable. It wasn't just the thought of things being there one minute – living, breathing, *alive* – and then gone the next that frightened me so much. It was the thought of *where* those living things went that terrified me.

My mother had brought me to chapel a while ago, hoping that joining the local Catholic community might be an opportunity for me to make some friends. It had been an unmitigated disaster. I'd heard of the idea of heaven and hell before, and that had been bad enough. But at least I'd held out the hope that if heaven was for good people, and hell was for bad, then I might go to heaven with the rest of my family. After all, my father wasn't a bad man, even if he did drink too much at the weekend and make my mother cry with his mean words. And my mother would surely go to heaven, with all her hugs and patience and bedtime stories. And even I couldn't be destined for hell – after all, Santa came every year to leave me something, and even if I didn't get the expensive toys the other boys at school got, it must prove I wasn't *that* bad.

But chapel taught me something else. Chapel taught me there was somewhere in between heaven and hell, somewhere called *purgatory*. I didn't understand the details. I just knew that everything ended up there – good or bad – in that strange in-between state of uncertainty and suffering. That's why I didn't like dead things. I didn't like to think of that place where their lost souls were wandering.

No, not wandering.

Pinned.

The butterflies in the case had outstretched wings, but their bodies were fastened to the backing cards with long, sharp pins that sliced through their thoraxes, holding their dead carcasses in place for all eternity.

I turned away, feeling sick to my stomach.

And that's when I heard it.

The sound of the butterflies screaming.

It was a soft sound at first, easily confused with the whine of the projector as the reel stuck and the mechanism strained against its mountings. The light flickered against the wall, the image of a caterpillar tearing from its black cocoon superimposed eerily against a blood-red butterfly with outstretched wings.

Then the noise intensified, breaking into individual howls that seemed to come simultaneously from both the display cases and the flaring light on the wall. The overlapping images flashed black, red, black, red, red, *red*, the butterfly disintegrating as the film spool overheated and ignited. Darks spots appeared on the wall, resembling melted faces with mouths twisted in torment, nails the length of spears impaling them and pinning their outstretched arms and writhing bodies to wooden crosses set in a lake of fire and brimstone…

"Jeremy?"

I looked up. My perspective had changed. Now I was lying on the floor by the butterfly cases, my mother's face hovering anxiously above mine. The stench of burnt flesh was still in my nostrils, but the only sound I could hear now was the hissing and clicking of the projector as the melted film reel spun on its faulty spool.

My mother helped me up onto shaky legs just as a curator came hurrying into the screening room.

"Is everything alright in here? I thought heard… Ah, damn it! That thing's always going on the blink." He hurried over to the projector and unclipped the spool, turning the machine off. "Just as well I caught it in time before it set the fire alarms off," he muttered, more to himself than to us.

"Come on, Jeremy, I think it's time we went home. You're overtired," my mother said, sounding weary herself.

I glanced around one last time before following her out. The projector light was off, the screening room dim and cold without its glow. The cases of dead butterflies stood silent and still, no sound but the curator's loud tuts to disturb their eternal rest.

And yet…

I was so sure I had heard….

That I had seen…

Overtired, that was it. I'd had too much excitement

and needed to go home to rest. And if I was lucky, when I closed my eyes, I wouldn't see those awful melted faces and hear the screams of the impaled butterfly-beings as they burned in the lake of fire.

2.

I wasn't the only one who was overtired.

My mother lay down to rest as soon as we got home. I went to my room, pulling out my colouring pencils and scribbling pictures of butterflies on the margins of my little notebook until the fading light told me it was long past the time when my mother usually made dinner. Glancing down at the pictures, I was disturbed to see that, without realising what I'd been doing, I'd drawn melted faces with mouths wide open in silent screams where the butterflies' wing spots should have been. I crumpled the papers up and threw them into the wastebin, vowing to think no more of the strange vision I'd had in the Museum's screening room.

I was just about to go and see if my mother had woken up and was starting dinner preparations, when I heard my father's key in the lock and the front door opening. I hesitated with my hand on my bedroom doorknob, waiting with bated breath. My father didn't like dinner not being on the table when he came home tired. How he'd react when he saw it was so far from being ready would depend on what kind of day he'd had, and whether he'd stopped off at the pub on the way home from work.

I heard his footsteps go to the kitchen, then a loud snort of annoyance. Definitely not a good sign. The footsteps crossed the hall again, heading for my parents' room. There was another moment of silence, and then a loud shout.

It wasn't the sound I was expecting. It wasn't anger or the beginnings of a noisy argument. This was a yell of surprise and fear. My hand gripped my doorknob tighter, the nervous anticipation at the pit of my stomach blossoming into full-blown terror. I froze, my fingers refusing to turn the handle and open the door. If I left the safety of my own room now, then whatever awful event had occurred to cause the panic in my father's voice would become real. I sank down, pressing my face against the cold wood and listening to the unfolding drama.

My father had run into the living room and was talking urgently on the phone. I heard the receiver being set down with a thump, then the footsteps ran to the bathroom, and back to the bedroom. The noises that followed were frantic but hushed. I was about to get up and tiptoe out, when I heard my mother moan.

I froze again. It was a sound so like the one I'd heard

in the Museum earlier, it set every nerve in my body jangling in terror. Images of burning faces swam before my vision, and I struggled to breathe as the smell of charred flesh filled my nostrils once more.

It was the pounding on the front door that snapped me back to the present. It broke the spell my limbs were under, and I opened my bedroom door a crack, peering out to see my father rushing down the hall. Two white bags with red crosses flashed past, carried by the men who hurried into our flat. I waited, standing in my doorway and listening to the sounds and voices from the bedroom opposite.

I could hear my mother crying now. That should have made me less afraid – she wasn't dead as I'd begun to fear. But I'd never heard my mother cry before, not even when my father shouted at her on a Saturday night after a long session at the pub. I'd seen her face go white and her lips draw up tight. But never tears. Never the long, ragged sobs that echoed hauntingly down the hall. Consumed by fear, I could go no further than the threshold of my room, not even when one of the men left, coming back minutes later pushing a stretcher into our flat. My mother didn't look at me or reach out her hand as she was rolled down the hall under a blanket. Her eyes were on the bundle one of the medical men carried. The towel it was in was bloody; I could see stains already blossoming in the middle of my mother's blanket.

"Jeremy, wait here, I need to go to hospital with your mother."

It was almost a shock to hear my father address me. I'd been ignored for so long I'd expected the macabre procession to pass down to the ground floor below without anyone looking back at me. My father hesitated in the doorway, as though trying to think of a way to explain what had happened, then abandoned the idea. He never explained things to me. As expected, he just told me what was going to happen.

"I'll ask Rita from next door to come and stay tonight until I get back. I need you to behave while I'm gone."

It was a pointless request. I was always on my best behaviour when old Rita was around. If I didn't do exactly what she said, she'd make up a story to tell my father when he got home, and the stern expression on his face would be replaced with his leather belt.

From where I stood, hovering in the doorway of my room as though held back by some invisible force, I heard the stretcher clattering across the landing to the lift and my father knocking loudly on our next-door-neighbour's door.

There was a hushed conversation, inaudible except for the words, "It came too soon," and then my father was gone and Rita was inside our flat, her leathery, chicken-like neck poking out above a hand-knitted sweater and a cigarette hanging from her mouth.

"Have you had your tea?" she asked, looking past me to the dark kitchen. I shook my head. Rita nodded. "I'll put something on, then."

She wasn't someone to waste words on a small boy. Her gossip and smiles were all for the women in the flats below. Passing my parents' bedroom, she glanced in, her wrinkled face screwing up in an expression of disgust at what she saw. "I'll have to clean that up too, I expect," she sighed with a certain amount of exaggerated relish. She enjoyed playing the martyr. The more she was asked to do, the more she could complain to her friends in the lower-floor flats on bingo nights, and the more cigarettes she could extort from my father on his return.

"Don't go in there," she warned me, closing the bedroom door firmly.

I'd thought it was unnecessary, that I'd have no desire to go and see for myself what horrors that room held for the adults who'd seen inside. But, nevertheless, my eyes were unwillingly drawn to it as I followed Rita down the hall to the kitchen.

Somewhere inside, I was sure I could hear a soft sound, which might have been the sigh of the wind, or the fluttering of tiny wings.

"Is my mother going to be alright?" I ventured as Rita

set me to work putting bread in the toaster while she scrambled some eggs.

"I expect so," the leathery woman said, the hard edge to her voice telling me she'd have no time for tears if I decided to look for sympathy. "They know what they're doing, those hospitals."

I didn't ask any further questions about the baby and the bloody bundle I'd seen the medic carrying out of the door. I'd learned long ago that answers would come when adults were ready to share them, if they ever came at all.

I sat at the small table in the living room, playing with the food on my plate instead of eating it as Rita clattered about with the washing up, making far more fuss over it than was necessary for one bowl, a frying pan and the couple of spoons she'd used. My eyes were drawn back to the closed bedroom door again. I knew it was empty – I'd seen both my parents and the medics leave. And yet…

The sound was still there, so soft it might have been the swish of curtains in the breeze, or the intermittent swoosh of rain against the window. But I couldn't shake off the feeling that I'd heard that sound before, in the screening room, as the screaming butterflies strained against the pins that held them down.

After a lecture from Rita about wasting food and more disgruntled scraping of my plate in the sink, Rita banished me to my room so she could monopolise the sofa and the telephone on the side table. I knew she'd be there all evening calling the neighbours to share the gossip of what happened here this evening. But I also knew if I dared to listen in, my misdeeds would be relayed in an embellished form to my father once he returned, and that would lead to the belt and several days of sitting sideways to avoid even more pain in my stinging backside.

I closed the living room door behind me, making sure Rita heard my footsteps in the hallway and my own bedroom door closing. She had a laugh like dishwater being forced down a rusty drain, but tonight she kept her voice hushed as she called round the various flats, heightening the drama of the story she was telling. I couldn't make out her words, just a few exclamations of, "Yes, I *know*," and, "*Terrible*, isn't it?"

I didn't try to piece together the fragments. I just wanted my mother back, with her smiles and hugs and brown hair swinging in its shiny plait. I didn't want to hear about blood and sobbing and the red bundle carried away by the medics. Maybe if I didn't know the details, it would be easier to pretend something awful hadn't happened here tonight while I was drawing pictures in my bedroom.

I glanced at the paper scrunched up in the wastebin. I should've torn the pictures up instead. One melted face was staring back at me from the corner of a sheet, its open mouth seeming to quiver as the draught from the poorly fitted windows caught it.

Maybe that's what was causing the soft sound I'd heard even more clearly as I'd passed my parents' bedroom. Maybe it was just the wind.

But I needed to know. After a whole evening of uncertainty, I needed to solve one mystery before I went to bed, or I'd never sleep.

I waited until I was sure Rita was in full flow in the living room, then I opened my door again and crept across the hall. My hand was shaking as I turned the doorknob of my parents' bedroom, but I knew if I hesitated now, I'd lose my nerve completely. I pushed open the door, and looked inside.

I wasn't sure what I was expecting to see. After my father's panic and Rita's disgust, I thought I'd see chaos. What I did see when I flicked on the light switch, was a red stain on the bedsheets, and a crumpled quilt thrown on the floor that looked like it was also stained. I knew my mother wasn't dead, and Rita had said she'd be OK.

It's alright, I told myself, willing my heart to slow as I took in the crimson stains. *It's all going to be alright.*

Some items had been knocked from my mother's bedside table. Looking for some way to be helpful – to connect with my mother – I hurried over and began setting the bottles of perfume and hairbrush back in place, hoping she'd notice my efforts when she got back and praise me for being a good boy. She might even let me brush her long, brown hair for her if Rita told her I'd been particularly quiet while she was gone. That thought gave me something to look forward to, and I looked around for some other little task I could complete to prove what a helpful son I was.

I was just checking to make sure there were no clothes to set in the laundry basket, when I saw it.

No, I *heard* it first. The soft thunking, the fragile fluttering that had disconcerted me in the hall. That's what made me glance at the window.

There, flapping helplessly against the pane of glass, was a bright red butterfly.

I stared at it in surprise for a long moment. I'd never seen a butterfly indoors before, not one that was alive at any rate. Its wings were the same crimson colour as the bed stains, its antennae and wings twitching frantically as it sought a means of escape. It didn't want to be in this room where something bad had happened, that much was clear.

I looked around for something to catch it in. Sometimes in the summer, my mother would give me a glass jar and we'd go insect hunting in the park. I'd catch a ladybird or a dragonfly, and sometimes even a small butterfly if I was fast enough. My mother would let me put some leaves inside and take it home, but only for the night. The next day, once I'd had my fun examining it and sketching it, I'd have to release it again. This summer, I'd accidentally closed the lid too soon on a butterfly, trapping it against the glass lip of the jar. I cut one of its wings off, and the butterfly had fallen to the ground, flapping desperately with its one useless wing. My mother had crushed it with her shoe, telling me it was the kindest thing rather than letting it go on suffering.

I'd vowed never to catch another living thing again for my own amusement after that.

Now, it seemed, I'd been given a chance to make up for that unpleasant mistake. Here was a butterfly that needed released, and I was on hand to help it find freedom. As carefully as I could, I tugged at the sash window, trying to pull it up a few inches to give the butterfly a chance to fly out. The heavy wooden frame was stiff, rattling as I heaved with all my might.

"Jeremy? What are you doing?"

I froze as I heard Rita's voice calling from the living room.

"Just going to the toilet!" I called back, hoping my voice sounded like it was coming from the bathroom next door.

"Straight back to your room after, then!" Rita called back. I waited, the tension in my belly easing when

I heard her going back to her phone call. I'd have to be quick or she'd come to see if I really was back in bed.

I strained against the wooden frame again, succeeding in lifting it a few inches from the sill. A cool breeze swept through the room, making me shiver. The light hanging on a bare flex above my parents' bed buzzed suddenly, flickering as though it was in danger of being blown out by the cold wind, even though it was an electric bulb and not a candle flame.

The butterfly hit against the window frame even more desperately, feeling the means of escape somewhere nearby, but not understanding how to reach it. I tried guiding it to the opening with the edge of the curtain, but that just made it fly even higher up to escape the encroaching fabric.

Next door, I heard Rita put the phone down with a clunk. She'd spent long enough there to call everyone she knew. If there was no one else on the list, she'd be coming to check on me before lighting another cigarette. If she caught me in here, it would mean an indignant story relayed to my father on his return. But it wasn't the thought of the belt that I dreaded. It was the certainty that Rita would look at the butterfly in disgust, before grabbing my mother's slipper from under her bed and crushing it with one blow against the windowpane.

I hesitated, knowing there was only one more thing

I could try. It was risky. I'd already made a mistake this summer that had torn a beautiful creature in half. But there was no more time. The butterfly had to escape *now.*

I brought both hands slowly up behind the desperately beating wings, and brought them together as fast and as gently as I could. I could feel a tickling sensation as the butterfly went wild in the dark hollow of my hands, its wings and legs trembling against my cold skin. I stretched my arms as far out of the window as I could reach, and opened my hands, praying that I hadn't done any damage.

For a moment, nothing happened. I was afraid I'd accidentally crushed the wings against my palms and the small creature had lost its ability to fly.

But it was just reassessing its surroundings. A moment later it took off, the red wings disappearing into the black night sky. The wind seemed to die down immediately, a soft sigh sounding in the sudden silence between the whooshing of cars past the junction. Then the traffic lights turned green, and the rush of wind was replaced by the jarring honking of horns and the revving of engines.

Next door I heard Rita stand up and cross the living room.

There was no time to close the window. I could only hope Rita wouldn't notice it hadn't been open earlier when she'd looked inside.

I raced back to my own room, clambering into bed just in time as my door opened and Rita poked her head through the door.

"Light off. Time to sleep," she said. She'd spent two hours on the phone to her friends, and I was dismissed in two short sentences. I was relieved. The thought of Rita's bony arms around my neck or those shrivelled lips coming to kiss me goodnight made me shiver in horror. I didn't want comforting words from Rita, or my father's gruff attempts at affection when he ruffled my hair when he was in a good mood.

It was my mother's arms I wanted, my mother's soft embrace and silky hair brushing my cheek as she tucked me in for the night.

They said she'd be alright, I told myself as Rita switched my light off and closed my door with a thump that told me opening it again before morning would not be tolerated.

She'll come back, and everything will be the same as it used to be.

I knew it would. I wasn't stupid. I could work things out for myself. I knew now there'd be no baby monopolising my mother's attention or taking up space in my little bedroom. Both would be all mine from now on.

3.

I grew up an only child.

Looking back, it wasn't what I wanted at all. Not that I wanted a sibling, but I wanted my mother's full attention on me. That's not what I got. When my mother came home from hospital, she'd changed. Gone were the hugs and the bedtime stories, the trips to the park and the long afternoons spent playing board games when it was raining.

In place of the mother I'd once had, I found a tired, washed-out replica, as though she'd been through a photocopying process that not only stripped the colour from her, but reproduced her face with blurred edges that crumpled into soggy tears at the slightest provocation.

I was no longer an object of interest. What happened that night after our Museum trip was never spoken of again, and no allusion was ever made to me ever having a brother or a sister – I never found out which. But the full weight of the event was felt by its absence, leaving a heavy hole in our family life that no amount of forced gaiety on my part or drinking on my father's could fill.

We never went to the Museum again.

My father gradually dropped out of work, then fell from our lives completely when his bad habits led to an early heart attack while I was still in secondary school. Callous though it sounds, that was a freeing moment for me. Released from being the 'child' of the house, I took responsibility for my mother and the household bills, relishing the opportunity to become a man at the grand age of fifteen. I stopped playing up in school, where my poor behaviour had become the only way I could wring some attention from my mother through the distraught tears the headteacher's letters and phone calls cost her. I got down to some serious study, staying up late after I'd finished my job at the local takeaway to supplement my mother's small social security payment, and working towards my final exams with real purpose. I knew that university was the best way to earn a decent wage and give my poor mother the life she deserved – one without worrying over bills or fretting over her inability to hold down a job without depression and anxiety overtaking her.

I worked so hard, I managed to earn a scholarship to study accountancy. I wasn't any more interested in numbers and tax forms than I was in the other subjects I studied at school, except in a utilitarian way, as a means to an end.

And so I went off to university, choosing the closest one in the city so I could continue to live at home and make sure my mother's dinner was made for her every night. She ate so little that her sallow skin hung off her bones, and the chestnut hair I'd admired so much as a child had turned prematurely grey, her gleaming plait long since cropped into a frizzy bob. I fretted about her constantly, eschewing all clubs and social activities to ensure I could be home as much as possible, just so she had the reassurance of my presence reading textbooks at the dining table while she dozed fitfully on the sofa.

The main building of the university where I studied stood across the river from the Museum. A short walk through the park would have brought me there, but somehow, I preferred to stick to the benches under the ancient cloisters during classes, watching the seasons change by the budding and falling of the leaves and blossom from the cherry trees in the upper quadrangle rather than venturing across the park where I might spy the Museum's imposing towers through the tangle of elms and rhododendron bushes.

Although I joined no clubs, as I have noted, I did make one friend during my time at university. Gordon was another loner such as myself, but more comfortable in his own skin than I was. I met him one day in second year in the quadrangle, where he was examining a beetle crawling up the trunk of one of the cherry trees. He was completely oblivious to the stares and sniggers of other students who passed, absorbed in his own contemplations. I sat on a bench observing him for a long while, wishing I could be as self-sufficient as he was. While I no longer had to endure the increasingly cruel jokes of schoolmates in exchange for the safety of a group to walk to and from class and with whom to eat in the canteen, I now felt the absence of company more than ever. It made me long to stay at home with my mother, where at least I'd share the same physical space, even if my presence seemed to register as little on her consciousness as the rain on the window or the blaring radio from the flat above ours. I knew I had to endure the separation for both our sakes, however.

The last thing I wanted was to end up like my father – bitter at dropping out of university early and forever blaming me for the low-paid work he endured as a result, as though his decision to start a family before completing his own degree had in some way been my doing.

Gordon looked as though no such worldly cares even entered his head. He was utterly absorbed on that September morning when I first saw him, his long blond hair falling around his ears and tangling in the stubble he'd clearly had better things to do than bother to shave off. For more than half an hour I simply sat and watched, until something – I still have no idea to this day what – prompted me to get up and walk over to join him.

"Beetle hunting?" I asked, out of practice for so long

that I wasn't sure how best to begin a conversation.

Gordon seemed to prefer the direct approach. "Moth spotting," he said without looking up from his magnifying glass. "You don't usually see Six-spot Burnets this late in the year. This one's a beauty. Want to look?"

I took the proffered magnifying glass and studied the wings of the insect sunning itself on the trunk of the cherry tree. The blood-red spots stood out boldly against the faded black underwings, almost as though a small child had deliberately dabbed at it with a paint brush for decoration. But somehow, seeing the red and black juxtaposed on the tree trunk like that reminded me not of schoolroom drawings, but of a room of a completely different nature. A screening room with a flickering light, with faces melting into fire with outstretched arms pinned to wooden crosses and mouths wide open in screams...

"Not a fan of insects?"

Gordon had taken the magnifying glass and was studying my face through it now, looking for all the world like a young Sherlock Holmes on his first case.

I suppressed a smile at the thought, despite the sharp taste of bile rising at the back of my throat. "I don't mind them. I used to collect them when I was younger sometimes. I liked butterflies best, but..."

"But then you 'grew out of it'," Gordon finished for

me with a snort. “My parents are still waiting for me to grow out of it and switch to studying something ‘serious’ like physics. But I want to be an etymologist, out in the world looking at real things. I don’t want to be stuck in a dingy lab working out the spin ratio of atoms or calculating the luminosity of lightbulbs. What are you studying?”

“Accountancy.”

Gordon threw me such a look of heartfelt pity that I couldn’t help laughing out loud.

“It’s not that bad. It’s pretty straight-forward once you get the hang of things, and it’ll be decent money at the other end. That should mean I’ll get to spend some time at the weekend doing more interesting things.”

“Collecting butterflies?” Gordon asked hopefully. I hadn’t meant to give him the impression that it was a hobby of mine, but I nodded anyway, keen to pretend we had something in common other than our complete lack of other acquaintances.

From that day forward, Gordon and I spent most of our free time in each other’s company. He asked me out on bug hunts and bee trails which gave me more unadulterated pleasure than I’d experienced since early childhood, and in return I helped him file reports on time when his mind was elsewhere. I hadn’t realised how claustrophobic my life had become until I tasted the freedom that running across the grass with a camera in pursuit of a darting dragonfly or a buzzing wasp could bring. The only qualification that I placed on our arrangement was that I wouldn't join him on nature walks south of the river. Through the trees across the bridge, I could see the towers and arches of the Museum framed against the sky. They always made me shudder. I couldn't bear to be near them after that day which had changed everything.

Gordon accepted this strange arrangement with his usual good nature, usually opting to walk with me through the glass houses of the botanic gardens or through the rose-edged lawns of the upper park. I never mentioned what I thought I'd seen and heard in the Museum, nor explained why I refused to join him on the days he went out collecting butterflies and moths. And to his credit, Gordon never pressed me for an explanation.

Four years passed faster than I expected they would on a dry accountacy course, and despite her worsening health, my mother insisted on being there for my graduation ceremony. Seeing the gleam back in her eye as she told the neighbours who dropped in to check on her all about her son who was the first in the family to gain a degree, I didn't have the heart to put her off, not even when Rita insisted on joining her to 'help out'. The last person I wanted spoiling my big day was the flint-hearted old woman who'd enjoyed every moment of gossip she'd got out of our family's misfortunes over the years, but seeing as her forty-a-day habit had merely shrivelled her leathery skin further instead of sapping her strength, and as my mother really did need all the help she could get catching the bus, I acquiesced without complaint.

In the end, I was almost glad of her presence. When my mother collapsed in the quadrangle while we were taking pictures after the ceremony, it was Rita who called the ambulance, and Rita who sat with me in the hospital while the doctors tried to revive her. Gordon had disappeared off on a butterfly-counting trip to Norfolk instead of attending the graduation ceremony, much to his parents' annoyance, and so without Rita, I would have been all on my own when the grim-faced doctor came out of the emergency room at last and told me there was nothing more they could do and my mother was gone.

The next few days passed in a blur. Rita's presence in my small flat felt like unendurable torture as she bustled around, making funeral arrangements and cooking meals I couldn't eat while I sat on the sofa and stared for hours at the wall. But when she was gone, heading back to her own flat late each night, I felt the absence of another body in the room acutely. In the lead-up to the funeral I came to depend on Rita as my shield, relying on her to pick up the constantly ringing phone, take custody of the endless flower deliveries and escort the steady stream of neighbours into the kitchen rather than disturb the leaden atmosphere in the living room where I was drowning in grief.

Rita even managed to track Gordon down and make sure he was given the details of the funeral. Without any living relatives left, I followed Rita like a lost sheep into the small church where she'd arranged the service, barely aware of the murmurs of the other occupants of our high-rise building as they filed into the pews behind us. I didn't mind that although my mother had been raised Catholic and made an abortive attempt to bring me to chapel as a child, we were now holding the ceremony in a Protestant building. I didn't even care that Rita had bought the most ridiculously eye-catching outfit for the occasion, the flamboyant black feather in her oversized hat drawing the stares that I'd been afraid would be directed at me in the front-row pew.

I was numb to everything, floating in a trance-like state in which even the light filtering through the high stained-glass windows seemed too luminescent to be real.

I was only awoken from what had seemed like a strange dream by someone slipping into the pew next to me, on the opposite side from Rita. I glanced up, and Gordon's face swam into view. His blond hair was cut neatly, and for the first time since I met him, he'd actually bothered to shave. Somehow those small acts emphasised just how solemn and serious the occasion was. I couldn't pretend any longer that this was just a nightmare or some outrageous drama cooked up by Rita to give herself something to gossip about.

Gordon's haircut and freshly groomed jaw made it all real. My mother was dead, and for the first time in my life, I was all alone.

I clenched my fists, forcing my nails into my palms the way I used to do when my father beat me with his belt. I wouldn't cry in front of this audience. I *couldn't.* If I started, I'd never be able to stop, and I couldn't bear for my grief to become a public spectacle to entertain the ogling occupants of our tower block.

Somehow, I made it through the service and the line of hugs and well wishes from virtual strangers without letting the sob building at the back of my throat escape. Somehow, I managed to shoulder the burden of my corner of the coffin as we descended the church steps and walked through the gates, crossing the road to the newer gravesite the council had designated as a spill-over burial ground now that the old churchyard was full. Despite the fact that I was at the front of the procession, it was those behind who were leading, gently pushing and nudging me in the right direction. I could barely see through the veil of unshed tears, but it was Gordon – holding the corner of the coffin opposite mine – who let me know when it was time to let the coffin down, and Rita who handed me a rose at the appropriate moment to drop it into the open grave.

I didn't hear the vicar's words or the murmured condolences of the other attendees who trickled away in small groups to the local hotel where Rita had arranged an afternoon buffet. My eyes were fixed on the yawning hole where my mother's body had been laid, staring at the crimson red of the roses that was juxtaposed with the almost ebony black of the coffin. Something was tugging at the back of my mind, a memory of red on black I'd seen somewhere before. As a ray of sunshine broke through the clouds, streaming down onto the open grave, a sudden memory of light against a wall and blood-red wings replaced by black spots resolving into faces surfaced once again.

I shuddered, about to turn away, when a sudden movement in the deep hole caught my eye. Almost against my will, I gazed down, afraid of what I would see.

For a moment, there was a trembling among the rose petals. Something was stirring, awakening. Something was fluttering down there where there was no wind, something small with fragile wings which were opening for the first time.

Suddenly a beautiful butterfly took flight, its chestnut

wings such a rich, radiant brown I instantly thought of my mother's luxurious hair when I was a child.

The knot in my stomach loosened, the lump in my throat shrinking as a calming sensation of perfect peace enveloped me. For the first time in days, I felt like I could breathe. Watching that butterfly flutter over the grass in search of flowers – a new life born amid death – I had a sudden glimpse into the eternal, a momentary feeling of connection with the whole of creation.

The chestnut wings were my mother's. Her soul was at peace, and I was being given this small sign as a means of solace amid my grief. My jaw, aching from hours of gritting my teeth, finally relaxed into a faint smile.

The butterfly alighted for a few seconds on the freshly laid bouquet sitting at the grave opposite before soaring into the air, ready to join the angels in the heavens above.

A moment, later it disappeared inside a layer of green mesh.

Gordon had whipped a small net from his pocket, trapping the butterfly with a practised flick of his wrist. Before I could cry out, he'd carefully extracted it and pinched the butterfly's thorax between his thumb and finger, killing it stone dead.

With a scientist's critical eye, he held it up to the sunlight, examining his find, before sealing the dead butterfly into one of the envelopes he always carried around for collection purposes.

For a long moment, I just stood there, my jaw hanging open in shock.

I'm not quite sure what happened next.

I think I might have screamed.

Sensing fresh drama, Rita was at my side in an instant, asking what was wrong. But my eyes were fixed on Gordon.

"What is it?" he called, hurrying over. "Jeremy, are you alright?"

"How *could* you?" I cried, my mouth opening and closing like a beached fish gasping for water. "How could you do that?"

"What?" Gordon blinked hard, unable to think of anything out of the ordinary he'd done. "Jeremy, what are you talking about? What have I done?"

"You *killed* it! You killed…"

I fell to my knees, uncontrollable sobs wracking my whole body until I was doubled over, retching into the grass.

"Jeremy, please? For God's sake! It was just a butterfly!"

4.

That was the last time Gordon and I spoke for nearly fifteen years.

I stuck to my path of becoming an accountant, despite the reason for pursuing such a deary career now being gone. I didn't have the heart or the energy to change my plans. It felt as though the rails of my life had now been laid, and I was bound to travel along them.

There were some welcome compensations for this weak-willed acceptance of my fate on my journey into adulthood. I met a nice girl in my firm's HR department, and we hit it off despite my shyness around other people. After a suitably long period of engagement during which we saved for a wedding and a deposit for a house of our own, we then married, moved in together, and had a daughter whom we called Eva, after my mother.

Life settled into a pleasant routine of work and home, with all the usual ups and downs a relatively contented family could expect. I didn't talk much about my parents or my life growing up, but my wife didn't press for details, and Eva was content to be fed on a diet of fairy stories, and later, more substantial fantasy novels from the local library.

I'd almost forgotten the strange incidents from my past, when one summer, my wife and I happened to both have the day off work. We'd planned a holiday in the south of France for the second week in August, and this early August day was earmarked for packing so we'd be ready well in advance. But the rain was falling heavily against the windows of our smart four-bedroomed house, Eva was restless, and my wife was finding her complaints increasingly difficult to ignore.

"Let's go out, Jeremy," she said, throwing down the travel iron she was attempting to squeeze into an already overstuffed case. "We're all getting cabin fever in here."

"Can we go to the Museum?" Eva piped up out of nowhere.

A shiver ran down my spine. I wasn't quite sure why.

"No, pet, let's go to the cinema instead. Wouldn't you prefer that?"

"Oh, no, let's not sit trapped in a stuffy room for hours with other people's kids!" my wife groaned. "Eva's watched more than enough television this summer already. Let's do something educational."

Faced with two sets of eager eyes and without a ready excuse, I could only grudgingly acquiesce. "Fine," I muttered. "I'll get my car keys."

"Can we take the bus, Daddy?" Eva asked.

"No! Why would we stand in the rain for hours waiting for an unreliable service then sit for ages on a bus that'll wander all over the back of beyond? I'll drive." I wasn't sure what it was that made me sound so impatient – after all, I was in no hurry to get to the Museum. But somehow, the thought of a bus ride on a rainy day in early August seemed eerily familiar, and I was keen to rid myself of the growing feeling of unease.

"A bus trip would be an adventure," my wife decided, helping Eva on with her raincoat. "I haven't been on a bus in years. We can sit upstairs and do a bit of sight-seeing along the way."

She had a look of quiet determination on her face that told me she'd already made up her mind, and no amount of protesting on my part would make any difference to her decision.

I went along with the plan reluctantly, refusing to look out of the window as the bus passed the junction where my old tower block had once stood, before winding through the West End of the city towards the park. Crossing the bridge, I felt an uncanny sensation of déjà vu, heightened when I saw that Eva had her face pressed eagerly against the window, watching the rain-swelled waters tumbling along the river.

The Museum itself was – mercifully – completely altered. In place of the cluttered exhibits, there were carefully spaced cabinets displaying objects grouped into modern themes. In one large glass case where I remembered stuffed animals growling out at me, there hung a high-vis jacket, a picture of a daffodil and a bunch of artificial bananas. 'Can you guess what these things have in common?' a cheery sign for children read.

"They're all yellow," Eva said, proud of her own deduction. The exhibit went on to discuss home-grown objects vs. imports, artificial vs. natural materials, but I was tired of real-world issues and was longing for the confused medley from my childhood by the time we'd had a coffee in the new café and made our way upstairs.

Some of the suits of armour were still there, at least, though I was glad to see the more grotesque medieval instruments of torture were long gone. Leaving my wife to read through the section on local history, I followed Eva as she skipped down the galleries, alighting briefly on each new exhibit like a moth drawn to a flame, before scampering off again. I was starting to crave a bench to sit down on, when Eva stopped, peering into a small room at the back of the gallery.

This time, she really had been attracted by a light.

"It's a cinema," she said eagerly.

No, it's a…" the words 'screening room' were on my lips, when I looked at the sign.

'Screaming Room' they said.

I blinked hard, my mouth turning suddenly dry.

When I looked again, the letters had rearranged themselves. The sign very definitely said, 'Screening Room'.

"There's nothing in there, Eva," I said firmly, taking her hand. "Let's go back downstairs."

"But I want to watch the film!" Eva pouted, wriggling out of my grip with that eel-like suppleness that all small children seem to possess.

Before I could chase after her, another voice close by called, "Jeremy!"

I turned. Gordon was standing at the top of the stairs, a clipboard in his hands.

"What are you doing here?" I asked. I wasn't sure how I felt about seeing him. Part of me was thrilled. He'd been the best friend I ever had. And yet…

The sight of him awakened unwelcome memories of my mother's funeral, recollections that brought to mind other unpleasant remembrances buried even further in the past, of the room before me and what I'd seen in there. I hesitated, torn between speaking to my friend and hurrying into the room to retrieve Eva and lead her elsewhere.

Gordon took my hesitation as an invitation.

"It's been years!" he said warmly, striding up to me and clapping me on the shoulder. His blond hair had quickly receded and he'd shaved it to make the bald patch less noticeable, but what he lacked on the top of his head, he made up for in the bushy beard that clung to his face like an explosion of moss. "What are you doing with yourself these days?"

"Accountancy," I said somewhat reluctantly, feeling momentarily that this answer would disappoint him. He'd never made outright jokes about my choice of studies, but he'd encouraged me to think about a career in biology many times during our nature walks. "It seemed like the best path. I'm married now – I'm here with my wife and daughter. Summer holidays," I added a little unnecessarily.

"That's great! I work here – I'm one of the curators. I mostly try to stop them from removing the insect exhibits and replacing them with picture boards and touch screens, but you can see how much luck I've had with that," he said somewhat ruefully, pointing at the room where I remembered the apiary housed in its glass case had once been. "They took the bees away last year – some vegan protest group said it wasn't ethical and we were exploiting them, or some other nonsense. They're coming after my insect collection now, and those little beauties aren't even alive."

Gordon paused for a moment, seeming to recollect something. An awkward moment passed between us, our minds both turning back to our last meeting many years ago.

I could see that Gordon was on the brink of an

apology, and I couldn't bear to hear it. To head him off, I said, "You should come and meet my wife – she's in the local history room. She'll be happy to meet you – she always says I don't tell her anything about my past."

A look of relief washed over Gordon's face. "That'd be great! Give me five minutes – I just have a report that I need to file first. Our online systems are playing up again, but I shouldn't be long."

He hurried down the stairs, gazing back up as he reached the offices at the end of the ground floor gallery as though checking to make sure I wasn't going to run off while he wasn't looking.

I had to admit, the thought had crossed my mind.

There was something so raw in that memory of my mother's funeral, so unresolved and so ambiguous as to its meaning, that I felt afraid of examining it up close. I hadn't thought about it at all since that day, just as I'd buried the memories of my last Museum trip deep in my subconscious. But Gordon was here with his collection of dead insects, and Eva was in the Screaming Room, and I had to face both.

No, the *Screening* Room.

It's just a cinema room, I told myself. *And Gordon said they were getting rid of the real-life insects.*

But they hadn't got rid of them yet. I could tell as soon as I walked into the small room and saw the cases up against the far wall. In fact, there were more of them than I remembered. Gordon had clearly added to the collection in his time as curator. I wouldn't be surprised if most of the new additions had been specimens he'd collected himself. Seeing Eva sitting in front of the cinema screen where a film of the life of butterflies was being played, I found myself heading over to the cases.

I wasn't sure why I wanted to see them again. I felt drawn to them, but in a different way than I'd been as a child. Back then it had been the lure of curiosity. Now it was something else – perhaps a desperate need to put the past to bed, to prove to myself that what I'd heard and seen that day long ago had just been a product of a child's overstimulated mind after a day of excitement.

I recognised some of the butterflies and moths in the first two cases from my previous visit, feeling pathetically proud of myself when their names came instantly to mind without having to read the labels. It was the final case that made me pause. These were Gordon's new specimens. He'd clearly spent some of the past fifteen years abroad. There were some rarer types that I knew were only found in the densest jungles and most far-flung places. But there were also a few home-grown varieties that I recognised from pottering about in my garden at weekends.

None of those were what interested me.

It was the small butterfly in the centre of the collection

that drew my attention. Its outstretched wings were the most luxurious chestnut brown I'd ever seen, its body pinned in place like the others with a long needle through its thorax.

I felt instantly sick.

It was the butterfly Gordon had caught and killed on the day of my mother's funeral.

"Daddy, the film's finished, I'm going to see what Mummy's doing."

I barely heard Eva's words as she skipped out of the room in search of something else to look at. I was left alone in the empty room, the light dimming as the film credits rolled. Against the black background, the names of the camera crew and producers stood out crimson red. I could feel the blood pounding in my ears again.

The soft music that had been playing over the film's narration had changed. It was no longer the breathy trilling of pan pipes. The notes were higher, more insistent. The sounds ascended in pitch, growing louder, growing rawer.

Screaming filled the room, bouncing between the butterfly cases and the flickering light on the cinema screen. The words blurred, becoming first the spots on the wings of butterflies, and then the faces of people that seemed to be melting down their skulls. The picture sharpened, and now I could see outstretched arms, nailed to crosses in a burning lake of fire. The smell of charred flesh filled the room, singeing my nostrils until I was dry heaving and gasping for breath.

This can't be real! my mind cried as I stared at the screaming faces of the pinned butterfly people. *It's all in my head! A child's memory of a dream, that's all!*

I tore my eyes from the screen and searched for the door. Eva had closed it behind her. I was alone with the screaming and the burning and the terrible sense that what was happening to the suffering souls was somehow all my fault.

Turning back to the screen, I cried out in horror. There was a woman thrashing against the nails that held her to a cross, her chestnut hair aflame and her terrified eyes pleading with me for help. Tugging with all her might, she pulled one arm from its mounting, half of her charred hand tearing away as she struggled to release it from the nail impaling her palm. She held out what was left of her arm, a motion both beseeching and accusing. Before I could take another step, the flames roared up from the lake beneath her, turning her into a living candle. The flesh melted from her face, running like wax down the cross she was pinned to.

That was when I started screaming too.

My terrified cries echoed through the room and into the corridor beyond, bringing footsteps running. After a few moments of almost insensible terror, I felt strong hands reaching under my arms, helping me to the benches where I slumped down, trembling.

"Jeremy! What happened?"

Gordon was gazing at me in wide-eyed concern. Behind him, the last of the film credits were rolling, the red letters standing out crisply against the black background.

"The screaming!" I gasped out. "The butterflies.... screaming!"

"The screening?" Jeremy looked round at the film on the wall, then turned his puzzled gaze back to me. "What about the screening of the butterflies?"

"You have to unpin them!" I managed to force out between teeth chattering so hard with fear I could barely speak. "You have to let them all go free."

"Free? Jeremy, they're dead," Gordon said in that matter-of-fact way he'd always had. "And anyway, they've already been sold at auction. The buyer's courier service is coming to collect them this afternoon."

"Buyer?" I gasped out. "But the other cabinet – the new one, those are your butterflies, aren't they? Let me have the brown one, please, Gordon!"

"Sorry, Jeremy, but the buyer particularly wanted that case. I can't take anything out or I'd lose my job. But if you're interested in butterflies, we can go collecting, like we used to – remember? I'll find you a brown one the same as that specimen, or like it, at least.

What do you say?"

I gazed up at my former friend's face, so innocent, so lacking in understanding of what he and thousands of other collectors just like him had done.

Forgive them, Father, for they know not what they do.

Those were the last words I heard echoing through the Screaming Room before I fainted dead away.

The Grinning Man

1.

Amy was bored.

She'd thought the trip to the museum would be a fun way to spend a Saturday morning, but as usual, her father sucked all the joy and life out of the visit. It started the minute they stepped off the bus, crossed the bridge, and walked up the grand steps of the old building.

"Don't push that!" her father ordered as she ran excitedly towards the revolving door. He grabbed the hood of her jacket, guiding her towards the boring side door that had none of the fairground attraction the spinning glass panes held for a seven-year-old child.

"We're not going in there," her father said firmly, leading her away from the enticing animal exhibits and marching straight to the Egyptian rooms.

"Don't touch!" he warned as she raised her fingers to the glass to trace the outlines of the jugs and bowls displayed in one of the cases. She shoved her hands in her pockets and tried not to fidget too much as her father took out his notebook and started scribbling away with his pen as he peered into each of the cases. She knew if she annoyed him any further he'd insist she hold on to the edge of his coat while he wrote, and then she'd be stuck staring into the same boring old case for hours.

Her father's work was important, she knew that. It had been impressed on her time and again for as long as she could remember. "Don't make so much noise!" her mother had always told her when she clacked her building bricks together in their plastic tub when she was three. "Your father's trying to write."

"Don't turn on the television just now," she was warned when the time came and went for her favourite cartoons. "Your father's working."

"Don't touch those!" her mother said nervously when Amy tried to make space at the table for her colouring pages by pushing a pile of her father's dry old encyclopaedias to one side.

She didn't know exactly what the book her father was writing was about, or why their family life seemed to revolve around it like it was a black hole they were forced to orbit, she just knew it was important. More important than her father getting paid work to help out with the bills her mother had to cover with the wages from her three part-time jobs. More important than making breakfast, lunch, or dinner, doing the laundry and vacuuming, or any of the hundred and one other household chores that all fell to her mother after her shifts. More important than going on family holidays – not that there was any spare money for that. More important than playing with Amy after school. More important than reading Amy bedtime stories. More important even than remembering to make the dental appointment for Amy that was long overdue despite the number of times she hinted that her tooth still really hurt three months after she'd first started mentioning it.

She didn't complain. She'd learned a long time ago that would earn one of her father's deep frowns and a look of such utter disappointment she'd be forced to question whether he'd really wanted a daughter in the first place. Late at night, when her mother was battling to put the house in order while Amy was in bed and her father was growling from his pile of books that she was disturbing him, her mother complained bitterly that he seemed to have been under the impression that he was merely registering for a library card when he signed their marriage certificate, and was disappointed to receive a wife and child instead.

Amy wasn't really sure what she meant by that. She just knew that ever since she could remember, she'd had to walk on eggshells around her father. He hardly ever paid any attention to her. He rarely condescended to engage in small talk without heaving an enormous sigh to show how tedious he found everyday life and how inane he thought other people were.

And he never, ever smiled.

Amy tried hard not to squirm restlessly as she stood – completely ignored – by her father's side. After all, it was her seventh birthday today, and she didn't want to be shouted at on her special day. They weren't making this trip to the Museum to celebrate her birthday, of course. Her mother was at work as usual, and her father needed to make more notes for his book. It had something to do with all the ancient objects in the cases, but he'd never bothered to explain what. Not in a way she could understand, anyway.

If she was good, there would be no harsh words before they returned home, and she'd be able to enjoy the special cake and present she knew her mother would bring home after work later that evening. She doubted her father remembered it was her birthday today. He hadn't mentioned it since he ordered her out of bed early that morning and told her to get dressed in something warm as they were going out in the chilly November frost. He'd let her have two helpings of chocolate cereal, at least, but that was likely to be because he already had his head buried in his notes and wasn't paying any attention to what she pulled out of the cupboards for breakfast.

Something in a case further down the room caught her eye. There were shiny blue objects in there, way more interesting than the dull browns of the broken pottery pieces her father was currently examining. Very slowly, so as not to draw her father's attention, she began shuffling sideways. Her father didn't like her straying from his side when they left the house. He didn't want her 'getting into trouble' and 'causing a fuss', whatever that meant. She wasn't sure what trouble she could get into or what fuss she could make in a boring old room full of things that were already broken and locked away in cases, but she knew the rules had to be obeyed.

She wasn't really *breaking* the rules by trying to edge across to another case, away from her father's suffocating presence. She was just *bending* them ever so slightly.

It was a relief when she finally made it to the more distant display without her father noticing. She was still on the edge of his field of vision, but far enough away that she felt she could breathe more freely, and at the very least, take her hands out of her pockets. She gazed at the new display with a fresh burst of interest. This one was colourful. There were lots of little shiny blue figures that looked like strangely dressed people with stripey hair. Some weren't much more than blurry blobs that looked like melted wax candles, but others were sharply defined, their features reminding her of the small collection of dolls in her toybox.

She knew she shouldn't touch anything, but she liked to trace outlines with her fingers on the glass cases of things she saw inside. It helped her to remember anything interesting that she could draw when she went home and was left to her own devices for hours until her mother returned to cook dinner. Her father wouldn't allow the television or radio on while he was working, and even the sound of her rummaging in her toybox set his teeth on edge. Quiet pictures made with colouring pens would be the safest way to spend the afternoon when they got home.

"Amy, what are you doing over there?" her father said sharply. She looked up guiltily. She hadn't noticed him striding over. At home, he could be heard tutting, sighing, and stomping from room to room to make it clear that every mundane task which took him away from his own thoughts for even a moment was an enormous effort and an inconvenience. But as soon as he left the house, he became eerily quiet, almost as though he was ashamed of being seen by the world. He wore his Trilby hat pulled low over his bulging forehead, further screening his weak blue eyes which were already hidden behind his tinted spectacles. He seemed to like late autumn and winter best when he could pull his scarf right up over his nose and mouth, completing the picture of a man so ill at ease in the world that he'd rather be invisible in public. Her mother sometimes muttered to Amy's Aunt Sarah that he was 'ashamed to hold his head up as he doesn't support his family like other men', but Amy didn't know what that meant. She just knew her father crept shame-faced through the world like a man terrified to draw attention to himself, and that put her on edge every time she had to leave the house with him.

"I'm just looking at these," Amy pouted, tired of standing still for so long and feeling put out that she wasn't being praised for her patience like she thought she deserved. "What are they?"

She knew her father didn't like small talk. But if she wanted attention from him, the best way was to give him an opportunity to show how clever he was.

"They're *shabti*," her father said, glancing at the cabinet. "A name possibly derived from the Egyptian 'Swb' – stick – or 'wSb' – to 'answer' or 'respond'. Those are made of faience. As conservation of the body was essential to the Egyptians in order to survive in the afterlife, they're usually interpreted as surrogates for the functioning body in case the deceased's mummy was damaged."

Amy nodded like she understood, feeling the familiar dull ache of disappointment that her father didn't talk to her the way she knew other fathers talked to their children. She'd seen those fathers at the school gates, picking their daughters up and swinging them onto their shoulders, or tickling them until they giggled so hard they were almost crying with laughter. They asked what their daughters did at school, and admired their finger-painted pictures as though they were more valuable treasures than the Museum held. The only time her father ever even glanced at her pictures was when he put them in the bin if they took up too much space on the dining table he'd commandeered as his desk.

"What were they for?" she asked, seeing her father's eyes stray back to his notebook and desperate to prolong the brief moment of attention.

"I just told you what they were for, Amy," her father tutted. "You need to listen."

His eyes fixed firmly on his notes once more, and Amy resigned herself to another hour of standing around with nothing to amuse herself but her own sad thoughts of how she'd rather be spending her birthday.

By the time her father was ready to go, she was weary with boredom and badly in need of the toilet. She knew she'd have to wait until she got home, though. Her father would be too embarrassed to take her into the ladies, and he didn't trust her enough to let her go by herself while he waited outside. He'd just tell her she wasn't a baby anymore and was old enough now to have control of her own bladder.

She was just resigning herself to the thought of an uncomfortable bus trip home as they passed down the long corridor back to the central hall, when something large caught her eye. She didn't know why she hadn't noticed it on trips here before; it took up almost one whole side of the passageway. It was a large stone sarcophagus in two halves, the smooth lines of the top half broken only by the carving of a head at one end, and the tombstone-like end of the other which represented feet.

Despite knowing she should be following in her father's footsteps, and despite her own eagerness to leave the boring old Museum and get home to the relief of the bathroom, something made her pause.

Even lying on its side, the sarcophagus was taller than she was, and she had to stand on tiptoe to try to make out the face that was gazing sightlessly up at the dim exhibit lights fixed above. The carving had the same elongated chin and strange, stripey long hair or hat – she never knew which – that the smaller figurines in the cases had. Putting her hands on the crack between the upper and lower parts of the coffin, she pulled herself up a little higher, trying to make out the expression on the carved face.

She couldn't be sure, but stone figure seemed to be smiling.

"Amy, what are you doing?"

Her father was very definitely not smiling. She knew that for sure, even though his scarf was drawn up over his nose and mouth and she couldn't make out his eyes past the reflection of Museum lights on his tinted spectacles. He came marching back down the corridor, already holding his hand out to lead her away by the wrist.

His sharp words would usually be enough to make her run straight back to his side. But not today. It was as though the stone sarcophagus had cast a spell on her, giving her the courage to disobey her father's rules. She turned back to look at it.

There was something eerie about the dark slit that ran all around the middle of the sarcophagus, dividing the two halves that didn't quite fit flush together. She couldn't see through the crack, it was too thin for that, but she was curiously drawn to the darkness beyond, almost as though it was whispering to her, inviting her to come closer and put her fingers into the slit and reach inside…

"Amy! What are you doing now?"

Her father tutted loudly as he took hold of her wrist, letting her know with as much vehemence as he could muster just how displeased he was with her.

"I'm looking at the stone box, Daddy. What is it?" she asked, hoping her usual little trick of asking him questions would distract him from the telling-off he'd been about to give her.

"It's not a box, it's the sarcophagus of Pa-Ba-Sa," her

father said impatiently.

"Star-cough-agus?" Amy tried.

"Sarco-phagus," her father enunciated more clearly through the fabric of his long scarf. "From the Greek 'sarx' – meaning flesh – and 'phagein' meaning 'to eat'."

"Flesh…eating?" Amy stared at the box in wonder. "Does it eat people? Is there dead people inside?" A shiver of pleasurable excitement rippled down her spine at the grisly thought.

"Don't be ridiculous." Her father was in no mood to humour her childish notions. "There's nothing in it. His mummy's not in there – it's empty."

Are you sure? a little voice piped up at the back of Amy's mind. She blinked, not quite sure if the voice she heard was her own. Whether it was or not, she had enough sense not to ask the question aloud.

Her father marched off again, and as his hand was now clamped firmly around her wrist, she had no option but to follow him across the central hall. Before they could reach the door, she caught sight of the iced cakes sitting in a display case at the entrance to the café section. There were slices of chocolate cake, strawberry buns, and whipped cream eclairs that made her mouth water. Beyond them, at the back of the café, stood the doors to the toilets.

Amy longed to be able to sit at one of the tables and

munch on a piece of cake the way the two children sitting with their own parents were doing. They were chatting and smiling together, the parents drinking tea and no doubt asking their son and daughter what their favourite exhibits were. She felt a hot flash of envy at how normal the scene was. She knew she could never sit down in a café with her own family like that.

Her father had a horror of being seen eating in public.

He wouldn't even sit at the dinner table in their own home while Amy and her mother ate, preferring to wait until long after they had finished so he could hide behind his newspaper and eat out of sight, as though he was doing something shameful. Her mother said it was because his parents were poor growing up and had made him feel guilty for every mouthful he ate, as though that explained why her father felt he had the right to tut in disgust every time he saw someone else eat in public. He picked at the food her mother spent hours making for him, but late at night, Amy could hear him getting up and going to the kitchen. In the morning, there would be crumbs all around the counters and the biscuit tin would be empty yet again. After years of secret bingeing, his body was so bloated that he could barely button up his bulky winter coat.

It was another one of those little quirks that Amy's mother had long since accepted, but which Amy couldn't understand. She hated the way that her family's every routine revolved around the things her father refused to do like normal people. Her envy of the happy-looking family scene and her longing for a piece of the chocolate cake she saw disappearing into the small boy's mouth made her unusually rebellious, and she asked petulantly, "Daddy, can we get some tea and cake?"

She pointed hopefully at the café with the hand her father didn't have clamped to his side.

Her father glanced round, and seeing the family eating at the table, let out a loud snort. Amy could just make out his eyes narrowing in revulsion behind his tinted spectacles as he muttered, "Don't be silly. It's disgusting, stuffing your face like that where everyone can see you."

Amy almost said, "But it's my birthday!" before thinking better of it and biting her tongue. *You'll get cake when Mummy comes home*, she told herself, confident that the voice she heard inside her head was her own this time. *Mummy promised. She always keeps her promises. Not like Daddy.*

2.

There was no birthday cake when Amy's mother came

home from work that evening.

It turned out that what she'd promised was to ask Amy's father to pick up a cake from the bakery on his way back from the Museum. There was an almighty row when she discovered her unemployed husband couldn't even be trusted with that small task while she worked shifts on two different Saturday jobs. Even worse, was the discovery that Amy's father had spent the money on a large tome of Egyptian history from the second-hand bookshop instead.

"You know I've been saving for weeks for that cake!" Amy heard her mother's strained voice from behind the closed kitchen door. "We can't afford both a cake and a proper present. She had her heart set on that fairy castle from the bakery, and now you've gone and blown her cake money on yet another bloody book!"

"You make it sound like I did it on purpose!" her father said defensively. "I forgot, that's all. I had other things on my mind. I've tracked down some really interesting inscriptions from the tomb of She-Rah-Ba dating all the way back to the Old Kingdom which—"

"I don't give a toss about your research! I'm so sick of this bloody book you've been writing for fifteen bloody years with nothing to show for it! What am I supposed to say to poor little Amy? She's been waiting all day for her birthday tea."

"Can't you just bake a cake tonight and she can have

it tomorrow?" her husband grumbled, as though he couldn't understand what all the fuss was about. "It's just eggs, milk and butter, or something like that. It can't be that hard. She's only seven, she doesn't know one day from another. Just tell her it's her birthday tomorrow instead."

In the sudden silence, Amy could picture her mother's face hovering between distraught tears and a full-blown meltdown.

Before her mother decided which it would be, Amy opened the door quickly, skipping into the kitchen with forced gaiety. "Don't worry about the birthday cake, Mummy," she said, giving her hand a reassuring squeeze. "I don't want one anyway."

She hardly heard her own words over the voice in her head pleading, *Please stop arguing. Please stop arguing. Please stop—*

"Now look at what you've done!" her mother said angrily to her father, refusing to be comforted by her daughter. "She's too scared to even admit she wanted a cake in the first place! What kind of a father—"

"She did get cake!" her father interrupted. "In the Museum café. Didn't you, Amy?"

Amy looked up, surprised. Her father had taken off his hat and scarf inside the house, and now she could see his puffy face clearly. In the stark kitchen light, she could even make out the expression in his watery blue eyes behind his tinted spectacles. If it had been stern, she might have been tempted to defy him. After all, it was two against one, and she had the full might of her mother's righteous anger on her side.

But her father's eyes weren't narrowed in annoyance for once. His eyebrows were raised, and there was a half pleading, half cajoling look on his bloated face. He was tired. He'd reached his limit for human interaction for one day, and she was scared if there was any more fuss he might end up gasping and clutching his heart like he sometimes did when there was too much emotional drama around him for his nerves to cope with.

"Yes," she lied, tasting the bitter words on her tongue in place of the fairy cake she'd been eagerly anticipating for weeks. "Daddy bought me a big slice of chocolate cake with cream." She picked that image, because that was what she'd seen the small boy in the café eating. More than ever, she envied the two children with their happy, functional parents who did normal things like eat and drink in public while making cheerful small talk about their day.

"Oh…" Amy's mother faltered, glancing from her daughter to her husband as though trying to work out why something didn't sound quite right. "Well, then, if—"

"Right, now that's all sorted, I need to get back to my work."

If Amy thought her lie on her father's behalf might earn her even a small nod of approval or an affectionate glance, she was mistaken as usual. He simply headed straight back to his pile of books without even looking her way. She was too used to being disappointed by him to be hurt by his instant indifference to her existence.

It was the next disappointment that really crushed her.

She hated being disappointed in her mother, but even more, she hated being disappointed in herself.

"Well, at least you can have your little present tonight," her mother said, hurrying back to her bedroom to collect it.

Amy stayed where she was, leaning up against the washing machine and feeling a warm glow of anticipation building in her stomach. Her mother knew how much she wanted the new Unicorn-Dream plushie all the other girls in her class had. She might only be seven, but she was already well aware of how little extra cash her mother had and how impossible it was to expect a brand new one. But maybe if she was very lucky, her mother might have been able to scour the charity shops on her way home from work and might have found a second-hand one. It wasn't a completely unrealistic hope. Her mother *had* been home late from work last Tuesday, and she *had* mentioned something to her father about stopping in at the Salvation Army shop in town before she caught the bus.

Everyone at school knew it was her birthday this weekend, and that no one had been invited to a party because she wasn't having one. That was bad enough. But what would be really embarrassing, was answering the questions about what she got for her birthday. She longed to be able to tell the other girls she'd got a Unicorn-Dream plushie, and for it to be the truth rather than a lie that would be exposed as soon as she started making excuses about why she didn't bring it into school with her when the others took theirs out at playtime.

Her mother came back into the kitchen with a gift wrapped up in recycled Christmas paper. One look at the small, flat parcel was enough to tell Amy that she wouldn't be getting a Unicorn-Dream plushie any more than she'd be getting the fairy cake she dreamed of.

She forced herself to look excited despite the churning in the pit of her stomach.

"I know it's not much, but I hope you like it," her mother said hesitantly as Amy unwrapped the gift. Inside the 'Merry Christmas' paper that was a month too early – or, more accurately, eleven months too late – lay a pair of gloves.

"I knitted them myself," her mother said quickly, not sure what the slightly blank expression on her daughter's face meant. "I found some sparkly red wool in the charity shop near the post office, and I thought it was just like the dress you said you liked last time we went past the party shop on the way to the supermarket that time – do you remember?"

Amy did remember the dress. It was scarlet and sequinned and sparkly. It had made her think of fairies and princesses and magic and all the girly things her father would tell her were stupid and childish and beneath his contempt. She knew the dress had been beyond her reach, but finding out the Unicorn-Dream plushie was yet another thing she couldn't have on top of the special fairy cake was almost too much for her to bear.

That wasn't what was causing the painful lump to swell in her throat, though. It was the thought that her mother had gone looking for something to make her happy, desperately trying to make up for her father's indifference. She'd sat up knitting for nights on end, despite how tired she was after work. She'd worked so hard to make Amy something special, and all Amy could think about was how much she'd rather have a second-hand toy from a charity shop than the gift her mother had put so much thought and care into making for her.

The gloves were a token of her mother's love, and she didn't deserve them. She was too selfish. But worse, she didn't want them even if she did deserve them. And that was what was making her bottom lip tremble.

Her father was wrong. Amy might be only seven, but she was far more aware of things than he gave her credit for. She knew her mother was watching her reaction carefully, and she'd be heartbroken if she knew how disappointed Amy was by the sparkly gloves she'd spent so long knitting.

And so she forced herself to smile and say brightly, "They're *lovely*, Mummy. I can't wait to show them to the other girls in school on Monday."

Her mother's face almost crumpled with sheer relief. "Aw, that's lovely to hear, sweetheart. I'm so pleased you like them. I know you wanted… Well, as long as you're happy, then I'm happy too. And I'm so glad your father did get you some cake today in the end."

"Yes, it was lovely cake," Amy repeated mechanically, the grin still frozen on her face. For a moment an image flickered through her head, of a stone sarcophagus smiling up at the ceiling, and she wondered if the person it represented had spent his whole life faking a smile too. Maybe he hadn't needed to fake it – maybe he'd been rich and could buy all the birthday cake and toys he could ever wish for. Or maybe he'd had such a hard life, that he'd been smiling like that because he died and finally got to rest.

Either way, she wished her father was considerate

enough to fake a smile like that, just once. She wouldn't care if it wasn't real. It would be proof that he could actually think about other people for long enough to do something purely for them, instead of himself.

Amy gave her mother a hug and hurried to her room to put the gloves into her coat pocket, anxious to get out of sight before the lump in her throat choked her and the tears of bitter disappointment began to fall.

3.

"Mummy said you'd take me to the park," Amy complained as they got off the bus at the stop by the bridge.

"I *will* take you to the park," her father muttered, "just as soon as I'm finished in the Museum. There's another display I need to study for my research. It'll only take half an hour. It's important, Amy."

And I'm not, Amy filled in the end of the sentence for him, dragging her feet as they crossed the road and headed up the steps of the Museum. She knew very well the Sunday morning trip wouldn't take half an hour. It would be two hours at least, and then it would be lunchtime. Visitors would start filing into the café and her father's lip would curl in disgust beneath his scarf at the sight of them eating in public. Then they wouldn't go to the park, because her father would insist there would be people eating at the picnic tables too, even though it was winter now and the only things eating food in the cold would be the squirrels and pigeons who fought over empty crisp packets and bits of Saturday night takeaway.

Her father's sweaty fingers dug into her wrist, pulling her away from the temptation of the revolving doors like they always did and escorting her though the boring entrance to the boring rooms full of boring exhibits in boring glass cases.

But Amy didn't stick her hands straight into her pockets when her father let go of her wrist and pulled his notebook out. She was feeling in a rebellious mood today. After yesterday's triple disappointment – her father forgetting to buy her birthday cake and spending the money on a book for himself instead, her father making her lie for him without even acknowledging it, and her mother's lovingly made birthday present causing her so much guilty heartache – she was in no mood to simply stand like a robot at her father side.

As soon as he began peering into the glass cases and taking notes, Amy began edging away.

She had a destination in mind this time. She wasn't heading for the cases at the other end of the room which were filled with little blue statues. She was heading for the corridor where the big stone box – the *sarcophagus* – with the carved face sat. Her father was so absorbed in his own thoughts, he didn't notice when she crept around the corner and darted to the tomb tribute to Pa-Ba-Sa.

Her heart thudded with excitement as she examined it under the special dim lighting. The stone was mottled yellow and black, the lower half of the box carved with strange pictures that had become blurred and indistinct over several thousand years. It was the upper half that interested her more, though. She stood on tiptoe again, trying to get a better look at the upturned face gazing at the ceiling. She was just tall enough to see it side-on, but she was sure there was a smile on those lips, despite the absence of expression in the blank stone eyes.

Holding onto the lower half of the sarcophagus to pull herself up higher, she felt her fingers slip, the tips partly sliding into the stone box. She leapt back instantly, her heart skipping a beat.

'Flesh Eater', she heard her father's voice say as clearly in her head as though he was standing next to her. She whirled round, but there was no one behind her. Her father was still in the main exhibit room scribbling in his notebook.

Amy turned back to the stone sarcophagus, crouching down and examining the slit between the bottom of the box and the lid. She must have been mistaken before. The gap was far too narrow for her to slide her fingers inside. And her father had said there was nothing in there anyway.

But still…

There was something mesmerising about that dark crack. Something which seemed to whisper that the stone container wasn't as empty as the sign beside it claimed. The longer she stared at the edge of the void, the more sure she became that the hollow space inside the sarcophagus was full of…*something*. Something equal parts menace and promise.

Drawn to it without knowing why, she slipped off one of her new birthday gloves and pushed the empty fingers through the crack, hoping to feel if it touched something on the other side.

Nothing.

The darkness seemed to swallow up the sparkle of the wool, leaving the dark red glove looking like it had been dipped in congealed blood.

Suppressing a shudder, but compelled by curiosity, Amy pushed the glove in even further, trying to find some little hint of resistance on the other side that might suggest there was something inside the ancient container after all.

Suddenly the glove was pulled right out of her hand, vanishing in an instant inside the sarcophagus.

Amy stared at the crack between the halves of stone in

shock. She hadn't dropped her glove, she was sure of it. She'd had a firm hold on it the whole time. It had been *snatched* from her. By *something*. Something *inside* the supposedly empty sarcophagus.

Before she could move, a voice behind her said sternly, "Amy? What are you doing here? I've *told* you not to wander off."

There was a dangerous twitch to her father's left eye behind his tinted spectacles that told her he was close to losing patience with her and her childish antics.

She ignored the warning. She was too upset to care how her father was feeling right now.

"My glove!" she wailed. "I dropped my birthday glove inside the starco— The sartofa— Inside *there*!" She pointed at the long crack running the length of the sarcophagus.

"What on earth were you doing something that stupid for?" her father snapped. "That's an ancient exhibit! You could have done untold damage! Come along, it's time you went home. You obviously can't be trusted to behave yourself outside the house."

He didn't suggest telling anyone at the Museum about it. Amy knew very well that the embarrassment it would cause would stop him coming to the Museum ever again, and that would be a huge blow to his research. His hand closed over her wrist again, hot and slick with anxious sweat as he cringed at the thought of her childish antics drawing the attention of anyone else.

"I'm not leaving my glove!" Amy wailed again, close to tears. "It's my birthday glove! Mummy made it for me!"

The thought of telling her mother when she got home from another long, tiring day at work that she'd already lost one of the gloves her mother had sat up for ages making was too much to bear. Amy already felt guilty enough for wishing the gift had been the mass-produced, shop-bought toy the other girls had instead of something homemade. She couldn't stand the thought of seeing her mother's disappointment at her carelessness.

"Please, Daddy! You have to get it out! *Please*?"

One look at his daughter's face was enough to tell him that Amy was close to tears. If there was one thing her father hated every bit as much as being seen eating by other people, it was the thought of causing an emotional scene in public. As far as her father was concerned, emotions were for Americans. The British had stiff upper lips, and if they didn't, well, they didn't deserve the paper their passports were printed on.

"Stop making such a fuss, Amy!" her father hissed, glancing around to make sure there were no other visitors in sight. "It's just a damn… Alright, fine! I'll see if I can fish it out."

He leaned over, his broad shoulders blocking her line

of sight. "I think I can see something in there," she heard him mutter. "I might be able to nudge it out with the edge of my notebook if I can just.... Ah, damn it!"

When he crouched down lower, Amy could see that his notebook had disappeared too.

"Now look what you've made me do!" he growled. "I need those notes. Why couldn't you just do what you were told? You're always so disobedient! I'm sick of all this constant childish—" her father broke off with a muttered curse, poking at the crack with his pudgy fingers and trying to catch the edge of his lost notepaper with his fingernails.

Amy stood stock still, careful not to make any noise as her silent tears fell. Why was her father always so horrible? Why could he never be kind and understanding like other fathers, just once? Why was it always about him and what he needed?

I'm not disobedient! Amy sobbed to herself. *I'm not bad. I always do what I'm told. Nearly always. Why can't you just smile at me, even once, instead of being mean?*

"Bloody hell!"

Before she could wipe her eyes, her father turned to look at her. His eyes behind his tinted lenses were wide with shock, and his scarf had slipped down to reveal his mouth pulled up in a frightened grimace. But not because of her tears. He didn't even notice those.

"Amy, my fingers are stuck!" he cried, a note of rising panic in his voice. "There's something… I can feel it pulling…. Amy, quick! Go and find the curator!"

Amy stood frozen to the spot. She didn't know what a 'curator' was. And her father's sudden fear terrified her. He never showed emotion in public like this. *Never.*

She watched with horrified fascination as her father's fingers slid even further into the crack, until half of his hand was inside the sarcophagus. He grabbed his arm with his other hand and tugged frantically, his hat shaken off with the violence of his struggles, but it was no good. His hand was drawn even further into the stone coffin.

How is that even possible? Amy thought. She couldn't get more than the very tips of her own fingers through the crack, and they were tiny compared to his.

"Amy! Get help!"

It wasn't just the terror in her father's voice that finally forced Amy's feet to move. It was the fact that he'd lost all control over himself and was shouting at the top of his voice. Anyone could hear him. Anyone could come and watch him make a public fool of himself with his scarf slipped off his face and his hat fallen off and his emotions on full view to the public. He didn't care now. And that's what scared Amy more than anything.

Amy ran blindly down the corridor, skidding to a

brief stop in the central hall and turning in dizzying circles as she searched for an adult to speak to. There had been a young woman at the café, but with lunchtime being a few hours away, there were no customers yet, and she'd disappeared back to the kitchen. Amy looked up at the first floor, hoping to catch a glimpse of another family, but although she could hear voices echoing up there in the distance, she couldn't locate the source.

The front desk!

She was sure she remembered there being an old man sitting there when they'd come in. Yes, there had! She recalled now the frown he'd thrown her father when he'd seen him dragging her by the wrist towards the Egyptian rooms.

She raced to the front of the hall, reaching the desk just in time to see the man standing back up again after arranging a pile of leaflets under the counter.

"Please can you help me?" she said, her voice shaking. "It's my Daddy! He's got stuck!"

"Stuck?" the old man frowned. "Where's he stuck, love? In the toilets? Can he not get the door open?"

"No, not in the toil-toilets," Amy wailed in frustration as she tripped over her words in her haste to get them out. "In the Egypt stuff, in the big box. He's stuck in the starko— The sharka— Please just come and help him get out!" she finished in a rush.

None the wiser, but reacting to her panic, the man threw his leaflets down and came hurrying after her.

"Stuck in the big box?" he asked as she led him to the Egyptian exhibits. "What big box? There aren't any boxes in there, and the cases are all locked. What do you—"

They turned into the long corridor, and Amy stopped dead.

Her father was standing up now, staring down at the carved face on the lid of the sarcophagus.

At least, she *thought* it was her father. Right up until the point he turned around when the old man asked, "Everything all right here?"

There was silence for a moment, and then Amy's father's lips drew up in a wide smile. She could see it clearly, as his scarf had now been wrapped tightly around his face in a different place. Instead of covering his mouth and nose the way he usually preferred to wear it in public, it was tied almost like a bandage around the bridge of nose and his chin, leaving his mouth visible. The skin around his mouth and tinted spectacles looked strangely yellow and wrinkled, but Amy thought that might just be from the dim museum lighting above the sarcophagus.

"Everything's just fine," her father said, his usually stern voice coming out soft and whispery, as though he hadn't used his lungs in a long time.

"Is this your daughter? She said you got stuck… somewhere," the desk attendant said uncertainly.

"Stuck?" Amy's father chuckled this time, his tight smile drawn up even higher, almost reaching the scarf around his nose. "No, no. My Amy's just got a bit of a wild imagination, haven't you, sweetheart?" Her father reached out and did something he'd never done before. He ruffled her hair fondly, as though he was amused by her antics.

His fingers were long and bony, as though he hadn't eaten in a long time. What was even stranger, was that his clothes no longer strained against a hefty body. His coat hung around shrunken shoulders, his sleeves too wide for his skeletal arms.

"She makes me, laugh, does my Amy," her father said, smiling down at her. "She's smarter than all the other children at school – always has been. And you should see the drawings she does! A talent beyond her years. She's only seven, you know. It was her birthday yesterday, but we haven't celebrated it yet, not properly. We're going to the park, then we're going to the bakery to buy a cake and visit the shop to get her a Unicorn-Dream plushie. All the other girls have one, you know. Aren't we, sweetheart?"

Her father's smile climbed even higher. Amy studied his strangely aged face for a long moment, before nodding. "Yes Daddy," she agreed. "That's what we're going to do."

"Um, alright, if you're sure she's…" the desk attendant looked as though he wanted to say something about Amy's strange behaviour, then thought better of it. He walked away, shaking his head and muttering to himself.

"Here's your glove, sweetheart. Put it in your pocket so you don't lose it." The bony hand stretched out again, giving her the glove she'd lost inside the sarcophagus.

"Thanks, Daddy," Amy said gratefully, putting it carefully inside her coat. "Did you get your notebook?"

"My notebook?" Her father's head jerked, his hat slipping even further down his forehead that seemed to have more wrinkles than Amy ever remembered. "I don't need my notebook. It's time I stopped writing that silly book. I'd much rather play with you, Amy. Would you like that?"

Amy looked back up at her father. The smile never left his face as he stared at her with strangely blank eyes that looked like they'd been carved from stone.

"Yes, Daddy, I'd like that a lot. Can we go to the café and get some cake now?"

"Of course, sweetheart. We can do anything you like. Let's go and get you a slice of chocolate cake before we play in the park."

Her father held out his bony hand. Amy slipped her fingers into it, feeling how refreshingly cool the parchment-thin skin on his skeletal fingers were.

"We're going to have so much fun together from now on, aren't we, Amy?" her father beamed at her.

"Yes, Daddy."

As they crossed the central hall to the cake display in the café, Amy smiled up at the grinning man, never once looking back at the stone sarcophagus that sat in the dimly lit corridor leading to the Egyptian exhibits.

ET IN ARCADIA EGO

1.

The temporary Poussin exhibition couldn't be over fast enough as far as Dave was concerned.

Not that he minded paintings at all. Keeping an eye on the art galleries upstairs was one of his favourite parts of his job as a museum security guard. No, what he couldn't stand was all the pretentious tossers who queued up for tickets for the touring exhibits. The rest of the Museum was free, so they wouldn't be seen dead taking an interest in displays that were openly available for any pleb to gawp at. They might occasionally condescend to visit the upper galleries where the majority of the art hung, but never without complaining loudly about the tourists taking photographs and the children who roamed the galleries while their parents enjoyed a few minutes' peace to sit on the benches and play with their phones instead of paying attention to the paintings.

What these punters really wanted, was the exclusivity that came with the touring exhibitions' hefty price tag, that kept the young families and giggling teenagers out of the Museum's pay-to-view rooms. Inside the roped-off area, the ticket holders were free to gather with other pompous pratts to show off how many art books they'd read. Dave had a 'buzzword bingo' game going with Betty, one of the other security guards. It was only June, and he was already on track to win that bottle of whisky at Christmas. True, Betty had nine instances of 'oeuvre', seven of 'praxis' and four of 'liminal' on her card, and he'd only clocked up six 'pastiche's, three 'gouache's and a 'distemper' on his. But he'd heard 'lovely chiaroscuro' murmured fifteen times during the Caravaggio exhibition, and that put him well ahead.

"As you know, Poussin was a master of the classical French Baroque style," the petite blonde art curator-in-training was beaming at a group gathered around one of the paintings in a gilded frame. "And we're lucky enough to have one of his most famous works on loan here at our Museum."

Dave checked his bingo card surreptitiously as she waxed lyrical about the painting of shepherds at a tomb in the countryside, disappointed to see that 'pastoral' and 'quintessential' weren't on it. Those words were too common to bother with. The group nodded sagely as she pointed out the main features of the well-known painting, adding their own little snippets of knowledge and congratulating themselves on how cultured they were.

Dave didn't know what all the fuss was about. True,

the painting was attractive – the sunlit yellows and idyllic blue sky behind the trees made for a pleasing contrast to the rather claustrophobic atmosphere of the windowless display room. But he'd seen too many pictures of half-naked shepherds and rosy-cheeked shepherdesses to be impressed by yet another one.

"And of course, this painting, as you all know, has a much deeper meaning than first impressions might suggest," continued Holly, the enthusiastic young trainee curator. "Take the fact that the athletically built shepherds in the peak of health are pointing to a tomb inscribed with the painting's title…"

Dave grinned as he got to cross off 'momento mori' on his bingo card while she talked. He knew that the painting was a reminder of death, and the title meant 'Even in Arcadia, there am I', and not just because this was the fourth day in a row he'd had to listen to Holly's breathless spiel about the overrated painting. He'd been working at the Museum for years – long enough to know the meaning of all the art terms better than most of the visitors did, not that they'd ever bother asking his opinion. There was something about putting on a uniform that made him curiously invisible to others, almost as if he became a non-person the minute he donned the dark blue shirt and trousers that set him apart from the preppy-clothed curators with their eclectic mix of posh accents and nose studs.

Dave shifted uncomfortably on his aching feet as the group moved on and Holly began another breezy exposition of the next painting. He'd much rather be upstairs in the free galleries, giving small children a ticking off for running down the corridors and glowering at students who dared to unwrap chocolate bars within ten feet of the paintings. He had some authority up there, at least. Down here, he felt like just another overlooked exhibit.

Two more days of supervising these smug twats, then I'm back on the night shift again, Dave told himself, watching ten pairs of eyes slide off him as the next tour group entered the room without a single one of them acknowledging his existence with a simple 'hello'.

Dave couldn't wait.

2.

"What you got there, Alice?" Dave asked when he made a last check of the Museum storage room at the end of his shift.

"New acquisition," Alice told him as she assessed the painting that had just been removed from its layers of glassine paper and bubble wrap. "What do you think?"

She stepped back to let him look at it.

Dave was flattered that she'd bothered to ask for his tuppence worth. He knew Alice was just being polite, but still, it was nice to be treated like an actual person by one of the fancy-degreed curators.

Dave liked Alice. She was in her fifties, same as him, and wore smart shoes and sensible twinsets. She looked like a proper museum curator, none of that pink highlights, fashionable trainers and tattoo crap the younger crowd all sported. He leaned over her shoulder, but it wasn't the sweet scent of her violet perfume that made him draw in a deep breath.

The painting was beautiful.

It wasn't by one of the old masters, he could tell that right away. It was done in a more modern style, but it wasn't some trashy piece of abstract art, the kind that always gave him a headache. It was a countryside scene, but he didn't think he'd get away with ticking the 'pastoral' box even it had been on his bingo card. The scenery looked more rugged, like it belonged to the Highlands of Scotland rather than some Arcadian idyll. In the foreground was a field full of wild flowers, surrounding a small pond at the edge of a leafy wood. Sweeping up behind were the slopes of majestic mountains, purple heather growing in the mossy patches between their crags.

It wasn't the rich colours and bright sunlight dappling the woods and kissing the meadow flowers that transfixed him, sublime though they were.

Dave felt a strange sense of déjà vu as he stared at the painting. The longer he looked, the more sure he felt that he not only recognised the scene it depicted, but that he'd been there before, a long time ago. Maybe he had. He'd been to a summer camp in the north of Scotland in his mid-teens while his parents sorted out their messy divorce. Maybe he'd even stayed at the very farmhouse he could just make out at the edge of the painting.

No, wait. He leaned further forward and shook his head. There was no farmhouse. It must've been a trick of the light that made him think there was.

"Well?" Alice asked, making no attempt to move away despite the fact that he was now almost resting his head on her shoulder as he gazed at the mesmerizing painting.

"It's a real beauty," Dave whistled. "That's going to draw the crowds for sure."

"I hope so. The budget's getting cut again this year, and the free sections of the art galleries aren't attracting enough people to justify their cost," Alice frowned. "The Director's making noises about selling off some of the paintings."

"The Director," Dave said fiercely, "is a complete plonker. If you were in charge, this place would be running smoothly, and there wouldn't be any talk of getting rid of the best exhibits."

Alice turned to smile at him, and Dave stepped back, aware he was standing a little closer than was polite. Her frizzy brown bob brushed his cheek, and he resisted the urge to tuck her hair behind one ear, not wanting to overstep any boundaries. He couldn't be sure, but he thought Alice might be blushing behind the thick layer of foundation she always wore, and he didn't know if that was a good sign or not.

"So, this is the last one you were allowed to buy this year, is it?" he asked as she turned back to wrap the painting up again.

"No, this one was gifted to the Museum through a bequest in a will. I'm not sure where it came from – I'd need to check the paperwork again."

She didn't move towards her desk, though, and Dave wasn't sure if that meant she was dismissing him, or whether it was because she preferred to stay where she was currently standing, side by side with him at the worktable with their elbows touching.

Feeling tongue-tied and not wanting to overstay his welcome, Dave reluctantly said goodbye, kicking himself for not being able to think of anything more to keep the conversation going. He'd been looking forward to the end of his shift all day, but now he'd much rather be working overtime if it meant he could have a few more minutes in the storage room with Alice.

There was a little voice at the back of his head that said it wasn't just the violet-perfumed curator he wanted to stand looking at a little longer, but he ignored it. It was just a painting, he'd seen thousands of them by now, and he knew the novelty would no doubt wear off during the countless hours he'd be staring at it over the coming months.

But still, it was a beauty, and he was sure he'd seen that pond and those trees somewhere before…

Stopping at the door, Dave turned back for a moment.

"Um, Alice?" He cleared his throat.

"Yes, Dave?" Alice looked up, her brown eyes large and owlish behind her tortoiseshell-framed spectacles.

"Um, I wondered if you might like to… If you'd be free to…" Dave fumbled for the words, the voice of doubt in his head reminding him that she was a curator, and he was just a lowly security guard.

"Yes?"

Alice was looking at him expectantly now. His tongue felt even tighter than before.

"Um, nothing. Have a good evening. I'm on the night shift from Monday. I might see you at the end of your day shift, but if not, well…enjoy your week."

"Oh. OK then. See you later, Dave."

He couldn't be sure, but he thought Alice looked disappointed as he closed the door.

3.

Dave didn't see Alice at the end of her Monday shift. He started too late to catch her, the Museum already closed up and the night lights on by the time he arrived.

What he did see, however, was the new painting. It had already been hung in one of the upper galleries, among the collection of Scottish artists.

Free to enjoy the peace and quiet of the empty Museum on his rounds, he'd decided to take a leisurely stroll through the galleries before sitting down at the CCTV monitors with Andy to share a flask of coffee. As soon as he entered the Scottish gallery, the new painting seemed to beckon to him, almost as though there was a golden glow emanating from the canvas.

Must just be the lights hitting the frame at a funny angle, Dave thought, glancing up at the dim night lights and not entirely convincing himself that his theory was sound.

Standing before the painting and able to see it at eye level this time, he got an even stronger sense of déjà vu. It rippled over his skin, raising the hairs on his arms under his navy uniform and tingling down his spine.

I've been there before, Dave thought to himself again. He was sure of it this time. He tore his eyes from the canvas momentarily to check the small description hung beside it.

'Landscape painting – possibly Scottish Highlands, c.1970s. Unknown Artist.'

That wasn't much to go on, but it did confirm that there was a possibility it was the very farm he'd stayed at the summer he turned sixteen. After all, the farmhouse in the corner of the painting looked exactly the same, and the woods…

Wait.

Dave looked at the painting more closely again. There was no farmhouse. But he was sure he'd just seen…

Confused and flustered by his mistake, he did something he'd never normally do. Something he'd *never* done in the twenty-eight years he'd been working at the Museum. Something he barked at students not to do, scolded small children for attempting, and lectured parents to keep a careful eye out for.

He reached out and touched the painting.

As soon as his hand brushed the edge of the canvas where he thought he'd seen the farmhouse, a jolt like an electric shock ran up his arm. He winced, closing his eyes and snatching his hand back.

When he opened his eyes again, the light had changed.

Dave was no longer standing in the dimly lit art

gallery. Warm sunshine caressed the back of his neck, a gentle breeze ruffling the thin hair that he'd carefully combed across his head. His shoes sunk into a thick carpet of moss, and he stared around in disbelief. He was in a meadow, patches of wild flowers swaying in clumps all the way up to the banks of a small pond. Beyond the dense woodland that lay on the other side, he could see the slopes of high hills stretching up to the blue sky, their peaks almost touching the fluffy white clouds that drifted lazily through the sleepy afternoon.

Turning his head, Dave saw the farmhouse. The whitewashed walls were just outside the frame of the picture hung in the gallery.

I've been here before.

He knew it with absolute certainty. Somehow, the memories of that summer had faded from his mind, leaving only a faint impression of warm days spent painting fences in the sunshine and pruning gorse bushes and apple trees. But he knew it had been the happiest time of his life, the time when he'd felt the most free.

Standing there in the meadow, he felt the same feelings of freedom and youthful possibility wash over him, flooding through the dry ruts his mind had become stuck in and purging him of the stale routines that had taken root like overgrown weeds.

He felt rejuvenated. Invigorated. As though he could

achieve anything. It was the same feeling he'd had when he was sixteen, before his parents divorced, before he dropped out of school, before he'd decided that falling in love and starting a family were distant dreams far beyond his reach.

Watching the patch of golden sunlight drift across the meadow as the sun slowly went down, he realised that's what he'd been chasing his whole life without knowing it. That patch of sunlight. That warm glow of light and life that he'd experienced in his youth and had never been able to recapture. But it wasn't too late. The gleam of promise was still there, hovering just out of reach. All he had to do was run and claim it, and it would be his.

It was only when he turned to look back towards the farmhouse, that he realised how dark the rest of the world had become. Apart from the single ray of rapidly disappearing sunlight, the meadow was being slowly consumed by the shadow of falling night. The farmhouse was already standing dark and cold as a tombstone, no welcoming light in its sombre windows to relieve its forbidding presence. The wood was no longer a place of enticing adventure, but a mass of tangled trees that creaked ominously around the banks of the small pond.

The surface of the water was a black mirror, absorbing the light instead of reflecting it. Despite the night wind that rippled through the grass, setting the flower stalks trembling and chilling Dave to the bone, he could see no movement on the pond, almost as though it was frozen in time.

Waiting.

Suddenly the dark surface shivered, parting at the centre of the pond. Something was moving in the murky water, rising up to meet the deepening night as it closed in on Dave from all sides.

No, not all sides – there was still that last ray of sunlight up ahead as the rim of the sun quivered on the lip of the mountain peak. Filled with foreboding without knowing why, Dave raced across the meadow, knowing only that he had to catch the patch of sunlight before it vanished and left him alone in the darkness.

Just before the ray disappeared, Dave managed to reach it, an electric feeling of warmth quivering through his body as he passed through the golden glow. His eyes were dazzled for a moment, and when he opened them again, he was no longer standing in the meadow.

He was standing *before* the meadow, gazing at the painting hanging on the wall of the gallery. Dave blinked in the dim Museum lights, feeling disorientated. He must have fallen asleep on his feet, that was it. It had never happened before, but perhaps he was getting old faster than he wanted to admit.

Not so old that I can't still change, he caught himself thinking. The memory of promise and possibility in that golden patch of sunlight lingered at the back of his mind, tempting him to be bold, to seize the chance of happiness and adventure with both hands.

Alice won't have gone to bed yet, he thought, glancing at his watch. If he was quick, he could still catch her before she went to sleep.

He was just turning away, when something on the floor beneath the painting caught his eye. There was a dark patch of water at the base of the wall, as though something had been spilled there. For a moment, Dave's heart skipped a beat, and he checked his trousers.

No, they were dry. He was getting old and might be falling asleep on his feet, but he hadn't lost control of his bladder quite yet.

Must've been one of those bloody art students, he told himself, pulling out the handkerchief he always kept in his uniform pocket. *Don't know how many times I have to tell them to keep their bottles in their backpacks. It's not the bloody Sahara desert up here, they're not going to get dehydrated if they go ten minutes without swigging their bloody mineral water.*

The patch of liquid felt strangely thick and sticky, disappearing as it soaked into Dave's handkerchief and leaving it ice cold to the touch. He held it at arm's length all the way down the stairs, draping it over the edge of the sink in the staffroom as he went to his locker to retrieve his phone. He knew the number he typed in by heart. It had been niggling away at him every day since he'd seen it on a personnel form in the main office. He'd wanted to it call it for years, but he'd never had the courage until now.

A memory of sunshine spurred him on, tempting him to chase that golden glow as it danced just out of reach.

"Alice?" he said when the person on the other end picked up. "Sorry, I know it's late, but I was wondering, would you like to have dinner with me tomorrow night?"

4.

"So, when did you say you stayed at the farm?" Alice asked, picking at the overcooked pasta on her plate politely without putting any more of it in her mouth.

"When I was sixteen. I can't remember any of the details now, but it was up in the north of Scotland somewhere."

"Yes, we thought it was a Highland landscape, that's what we put on the label. You can't remember anything more specific than that?"

Alice was sounding disappointed, and not just by Dave's inability to recall the location of the farm depicted in the painting. The flouncy dress and bright red lipstick she was wearing were too showy for the small café Dave had booked, and the food on offer had been underwhelming. Dave picked at his own burger and chips, wishing he'd been able to afford that fancy Italian place further up the street, but knowing his budget was constrained by his need to pay the rent on his cramped flat that was already two days overdue.

"I can't seem to remember anything about that summer at all, except that it was sunny and warm and I had a great time on the farm." Dave speared a greasy chip with his fork, then set it back down again, his own appetite gone.

This was a mistake, he thought miserably. *What was I thinking? Alice earns three times what I do. She's used to eating in much better places than this run-down old dump.*

"It was probably the shock," Alice said, taking a gulp of vinegary wine and doing her best not to wince as she swallowed. "You know, of your parents' divorce?"

"Yes, probably." Dave gave her the first genuine smile he'd been able to muster all evening. He'd told her about his parents' divorce years ago at a Museum Christmas party when they'd both had a bit too much free prosecco. He didn't think she'd remember. He recalled everything she'd told him, though, about her failed relationships, her longing for the children she'd never had, and her estrangement from the sister she hadn't seen in years. She'd been cold to him for months after that party. He'd wondered if she regretted being so open about her life with someone like him. Someone who earned less. Someone who wasn't on her *level.*

But here she was having dinner with him and discussing details of his life that she'd remembered. Maybe there was still some hope after all, despite the cheap wine and the disappointing food.

"I was in therapy for months after that summer," he told her, taking a gamble that opening up more would make her overlook their unromantic surroundings. "I think the divorce must've hit me really hard, and I just blanked the whole period out."

"Yes, that happened to me when my father passed away," Alice said, leaning forward more eagerly now at the promise of shared intimacies. "I can't for the life of me recall the weeks after the funeral. It was like I was in a dream state the whole time. Therapy helped, of course. It's good to be able to talk to someone, isn't it?" Her smile was wider now too, and he saw she'd got a spot of red lipstick on her front tooth, next to the bit of stuck pepper. "Did therapy help you remember anything?"

Dave wanted to be able to agree with her, to prove they had something in common, but the honest truth was, the long sessions hadn't helped him recall a single thing. It was seeing the painting that had jogged his memory. As he'd slept off the night shift that afternoon, he thought he might have had a dream about something connected to the summer trip, though he couldn't remember it clearly.

"I think…" he said slowly. "I think there might have been a girl there. At the camp, I mean."

"A girl? Ooh, how promising!" Alice leaned even further forward, revealing a little too much décolletage for a woman of her age.

"It was nothing like that!" Dave said, laughing a little too loud to cover the fact that his eyes were lingering too long on her low-cut dress. "I'm not sure she was…"

"Was what?"

"I don't know – *right*, somehow. Och, I just can't remember. It was so long ago. Makes me feel old just thinking about it."

The smile left Alice's lips, and she sat back in her chair, pulling her pink cardigan over her dress primly as though she was cold.

Shit, Dave thought. He'd forgotten Alice was a good three years older than he was.

"Um, but couldn't you trace the location of the

painting through the family that made the bequest?" Dave asked, trying to keep the conversation going a little longer despite the fact that neither of them had finished their main course and the dessert menu looked even less tempting than the starters had been.

"Of course I tried that." Alice sounded put out, as though she'd been doubly insulted by an insinuation about her ability to do her own job on top of the reminder of her age. "It was a dead end. The owner lived in Glasgow and left the painting to the Museum in his will, that's all I was able to find out from the notes we were given."

"Oh." Dave felt the heavy weight of disappointment settle on his shoulders again. The glow of promise was fading away, reminding him that all he had to look forward to after his shift tonight was an empty flat and an irate landlord who'd now have to wait another week for the rent. "Um, well, anyway – would you like to look at the dessert menu?"

"No, thank you. I should be going – your night shift will be starting soon, won't it?"

Dave nodded glumly, wishing now he'd never given in to the temptation to try to change things for the better. Happiness was a mirage, and love a hopeless fantasy. He should have learned his lesson by now.

Such things weren't for the likes of him.

5.

He'd promised himself he'd stay away from the painting that night.

Dave managed to resist the temptation to look in on the Scottish gallery right up until his final walkaround. He'd done two circuits already, in between stints sitting at the CCTV banks. He didn't really need to sit at the monitors, as that was mostly Andy's job. But Andy was a lazy git who spent most of the night snoring with his head on the desk, and Dave liked to open the door of the monitoring room with a loud bang to scare the crap out of him.

Serve the sleepy sod right if I gave him a heart attack, Dave thought as he crossed the central hall on his last sweep of the Museum. *He doesn't deserve to get paid the same as me when he only does half the work. Not that I get paid anything to write home about.*

The memory of the dismal meal in the cheap café surfaced again, and Dave winced with fresh humiliation as the last few minutes replayed over and over in his head. He didn't have a credit card anymore – it had taken him years to clear the debts from the last one after paying his mother's care home bills, and now that she was gone and he just had himself to look out for, he'd promised himself he'd live within his means. He was sure he'd had enough to cover the bill, but he'd miscalculated. He shouldn't have had a starter, but he'd been keen to make a good impression when they first sat down, and Alice would have been embarrassed to eat alone if he hadn't joined her. She'd pretended she didn't mind splitting the bill, even though he'd only asked if she could cover one glass of wine. She'd pulled her card out breezily and smiled at the waiter, but he could tell by the way the vein on her temple pulsed below the layer of foundation that she'd found the whole scene as excruciating as he had.

Forget about it, Dave told himself, looking out of the front entrance and watching the dawn wax in sickly hues behind the grey clouds. *It was a stupid idea, and you got what you deserved.*

The weather forecast had been for sunny spells, but Dave was pretty sure they'd got that wrong again. They hadn't had a decent day all April so far. The only real sunshine he'd seen had been in the painting upstairs, the one his feet seemed drawn to against his will…

He checked himself before he reached the staircase, turning sharply and heading for the roped-off Poussin exhibition instead.

There was a reverent hush in the pay-to-view rooms, as though the very air was aware of how privileged it was to be sharing the same space as the famous paintings. The night lighting in here seemed to be tasteful rather than dim, reminding Dave of the kind of fancy restaurant he should have taken Alice to, if only he'd had the means.

All this wealth I've been guarding faithfully for years, he thought to himself sourly as he scanned the artwork, *and what have I got to show for it? There's blokes with trust funds and rich parents who don't work a day in their lives but who could buy up this whole exhibition with their loose change. How's that fair?*

He tried not to think of his own parents. His father had promised to pay for Dave to go to university if he got good grades in school, and a college course if he didn't. But after the divorce, there had been no more talk of that, and his father had disappeared off and never contributed a single penny to the family finances. Dave had to drop out of school to support himself and his mother, and take what work was on offer. He'd been lucky to get this job after years of flipping burgers and shifting boxes in warehouses, he knew that. He'd accepted it a long time ago. He didn't know why he'd got so restless and dissatisfied with his lot in life all of a sudden. It wasn't like him at all.

Bloody Alice, he thought. *It's her who's given me ideas above my station, smiling at me and making me think I was in with a chance. Should've kept my distance. Would've done, if I had any bloody sense.*

He stopped at the centrepiece of the exhibition, the

painting labelled 'Et In Arcadia Ego'. He couldn't help wondering how much Holly got paid to give the smug punters her spiel about the shepherds pointing to the tomb with its warning of death in paradise. He could give them the same talk in his sleep. But no one would give him a job like that. He wasn't young and blonde, with a fancy degree from a posh university and…

Dave's eyes narrowed. There was something familiar about this painting too, and not because he's seen it for five days in a row on the dayshift. He leaned closer, looking at the group around the tomb. It was the shepherdess, that was it. She had curly hair and rosy cheeks, a nose too pointy for his tastes. The folds of her gold cloak and blue dress suggested a figure too plump to be good-looking by modern standards, but Dave had never liked the stick-thin model look anyway. He liked his women – the women he got to look at, but hardly ever touch, he reflected bitterly – to be round, like Alice. Not that the shepherdess in the painting looked anything like the ageing art curator. She reminded him of someone else, someone from long ago. Someone half forgotten…

Christ, I really am getting old, Dave thought wearily, heading out and stomping up the stairs to shake off the weight of unwelcome memories that clung to him like barnacles on the ageing hull of a worn-out ship. He was sure if he prised them open there'd be nothing inside but darkness and emptiness, no treasures secreted away in the baggage of the past.

And yet…

There was golden sunshine still to be found there if he looked.

Don't look, he warned himself.

He looked.

As soon as he put his head round the entrance to the Scottish gallery, his feet moved of their own accord, carrying him to the painting of the Highland scene from the happy summer of his youth. There was no shadow to mar the glorious landscape, and the clouds were light and wispy, no threat of rain in the soft tendrils that grazed the mountain peaks.

I wish I could go back to that summer, he thought. He remembered now that he hadn't been told his parents were divorcing until after he got back. He'd thought he was just being sent on an adventure. Maybe that was why he felt such a longing for the golden glow of youth. And maybe Alice was right – it must've been the shock of his parents announcing their divorce when he got home that made him forget everything that had happened while he'd stayed on the farm.

Yes, that was it. The shock of the divorce. Not the other shock, the one that he'd buried so deep in his mind he could barely even recall…

Wait, what..? Dave thought, a sudden shudder running

through him. *What other..?*

He didn't get to finish the question whirling around his head. Without even realising his hand was moving, he'd reached out to touch the canvas.

The dim Museum nightlights flared around him, his arm tingling strangely. And then he was in the meadow again, basking in sunshine, revelling in the warmth of summer and beauty and youth. His whole body relaxed, the weight he'd been carrying around finally lifting. There was no regret over wasted opportunities here, no worries about money and no memory of petty humiliations to vex him. There was only the welcoming farmhouse, with the smell of fresh baking wafting through the open door, the picturesque woods, with birds twittering joyfully in the trees, and endless blue skies above him.

Dave lay back in the grass, his head cushioned by moss and his cheeks caressed by wild flowers. *This*, he thought as he closed his eyes and drank in the calming sounds and sweet summer perfume, *is paradise.*

How long he lay there, he couldn't quite remember. It was only when a chill wind rustled through the grass, that he finally opened his eyes again.

Shit! he thought, sitting up with a start. *How could I have lost track of time like that? How could I have forgotten what happened last time?*

Darkness was stalking the landscape, hunting the last

ray of sunlight as it drifted across the meadow. The farmhouse loomed desolate and foreboding against the black sky. The branches of the woodland trees tossed restlessly in the first strong gusts of the coming storm. The surface of the pond, though, was eerily still, as though the wind was too afraid to touch it.

Dave glanced nervously at the retreating patch of sunlight. There was still time to catch it. It wouldn't take him long to nip over and have a quick look, then he'd—

What are you doing? he asked himself as he found his feet leading him in the opposite direction to the one he wanted to go in. He wanted to chase the sun's last ray on the grass, not head into the deep shadows gathering around the pond. But there was something compelling him to the water's edge, telling him to look into the murky depths. It wasn't a physical force, but a mental one that seemed to come from inside his own mind, as though the lure of subconscious curiosity was so strong he couldn't resist.

What have you forgotten? a voice was whispering inside his head. *What was so bad it wiped all the memories of that happy summer from your mind?*

I don't know! he shouted back. *And I don't care! I just want to go—*

At that moment, a dead hand covered in pondweed snaked from the water and grabbed the front of his shirt.

Pulled off balance, Dave fell face-first into the pond. Icy water closed around him, forcing its way into his mouth, foul and brackish and tasting of death. He fought against the force tugging at him, kicking the eel-like fingers away and desperately clawing his way to the surface. He hauled himself back onto the bank, coughing painfully and shivering, his whole body aching with cold.

The darkness was almost overwhelming. The tiny patch of sunlight was so far in the distance across the meadow it seemed almost certainly out of reach. Terrified by the thought of being left in the dark with the thing in the water, Dave staggered to his feet and stumbled through the wind-whipped grass, desperate to reach the safety of the last ray of light. The moss that had been soft and spongy before, inviting him to lie back and bask in the sunshine, was now dank and boggy, sucking at his feet and slowing him down further.

As the ray of light retreated, the sun sinking to its last ebb behind the mountain's peak, Dave looked back over his shoulder.

What he saw made him moan in horror.

Something had crawled out of the pond to follow him – a figure creeping on all fours. The darkness seemed to emanate from it as it twitched and jerked its way across the grass behind him, drawing steadily nearer as the sun dipped lower.

Dave gulped down a last gasp of ice-cold air and flung himself at the patch of sunlight that had turned from golden yellow to blood red as the sun disappeared. Pain shot through him, and he couldn't tell if he was falling, drowning, or being torn in half as light burst behind his eyes.

Then everything went black.

6.

"Dave? What on *earth* are you doing?"

Alice stood in the hallway, her keys still in her hand as she stared at the shivering figure in front of her.

Dave was soaked from head to foot, his uniform clinging in the most unflattering way possible to his paunchy belly, and his thin wisps of hair plastered to his face.

"I h-had to get-t out," Dave shivered, his teeth chattering. He was missing a shoe, and his socks were leaving muddy pools on the marble floor.

"Out? In this downpour?" Alice gazed at the early morning rain pounding against the glass of the entrance doors, then back at the trembling security guard. "You're not saying you went for a walk in...

Never mind, let's just get you downstairs and get you dry."

She shook the water from her enormous golf umbrella, setting it in the staff coat stand and taking Dave gently by the arm.

He followed her down to the staffroom willingly enough, although he kept gazing behind him, as though fearful they were being followed.

"Don't worry, no one else will ever know you've been this silly," Alice said soothingly. "I'm an hour early, and it's only Andy on CCTV duty, isn't? That dozy sod will be sound asleep again, I'll bet. He won't see a thing."

She wasn't sure if it was his chattering teeth that were making him grin, or whether he found the thought amusing. Either way, she was worried about him. She'd been working at the Museum for almost as long as he had, and she'd never known Dave to be anything other than sensible and dependable. A little too stolid and predictable for her liking, if she was being honest, with his limited store of small talk used up once the weather and the previous day's TV had been covered, and his same three jokes he trotted out at every Christmas party.

But beggars couldn't be choosers, and Alice knew the boat had long since sailed with her fantasy Prince Charming on board. Besides, she was used to Dave, the same way she was used to the old cardigans she kept at the back of her cupboard because she'd had them for years and she couldn't bear to throw them out. The other evening might have been a bit embarrassing, but she should've known better than to agree to a dinner date without insisting upfront she foot half the bill. However unromantic she might find it, it was a modern world, and she'd been single long enough to be used to paying her own way.

"There you go, you sit there while I put the kettle on." Alice guided Dave into a chair in the staffroom, drawing her own coat around his shoulders. "Have you got a spare uniform in your locker?"

"Yes, it's alright, I can get it…" Dave's hands were shaking so hard he could barely pull the key from his pocket, never mind get it in the lock.

Alice took it from him and opened his locker, taking out his neatly folded uniform and telling him to pop to the loos to get changed before he caught his death of cold. She couldn't help having a quick rummage inside while he was gone. After all, she had put on her special lacy underwear for the dinner the other night, though what she thought that might be for she wasn't certain now, as she knew Dave would be working the night shift straight after. Maybe she'd just wanted the thrill of knowing it was there, to bring some romance to the occasion, even if it was just in her own head.

Dave's locker was as disappointing as his dinner date had been. Apart from the uniform, there was a can of supermarket own-brand deodorant spray, a pair of plimsoles, a shoehorn, and half a packet of breath mints. Alice closed the door, annoyed at herself for expecting anything more exciting. After being work colleagues for a quarter of a century, she'd be deluding herself to think there were any hidden depths to the plodding security guard that she hadn't already plumbed. At that Christmas party some years ago, she'd thought there might be a secret well of information, or some background tragedy that might bring Dave to life when he'd talked of his parents' divorce. But it turned out to be a run-of-the-mill story, with details so boring he didn't seem able to recall them clearly himself.

"Tea's ready. Watch you don't spill it. It's hot." Alice handed Dave a steaming mug when he returned to the staffroom, disappointed to find herself falling back into predictable patterns of speech already after the hint of something more promising that had been suggested by yesterday's dinner date.

"Thanks," Dave said, the colour beginning to return to his cheeks as he sat down again and sipped at his tea. He was still missing a shoe, but the sensible plimsoles in his locker would be enough to get him home, at least.

"So, what possessed you to go walking in the rain?" Alice asked, hoping for a more interesting answer than she suspected she'd get.

"*Possessed?*" Dave looked up sharply, his eyes wide.

"Yes. I mean, why did you think going out in that downpour was a good idea?"

Even though he was now dry, Dave shifted uncomfortably in his seat as though his uniform was clinging too tightly. "I... I just needed to see the sunlight," he said at last.

"What sunlight?" Alice snorted. "It's as grey as an elephant's arse out there!" Fearing that turn of phrase wasn't as lady-like as Dave with his old-fashioned ways might like, she said quickly, "I mean, there wasn't much of a dawn to see when I drove here. Were you feeling claustrophobic?"

She'd heard of people working in supermarkets and shopping malls going stir-crazy on night shifts. If Dave was having some sort of mental breakdown, it might not make him more attractive boyfriend material, but it might make him a bit more interesting as a colleague.

Dave just shook his head, staring at the floor and sipping his tea slowly.

Alice sighed to herself. As usual, something that started promisingly with Dave just fizzled out into everyday, humdrum routine.

She was just about to get up and go to her office to

start work, when Dave said suddenly, "You know that thing you were asking me last night?"

"Yes?" Alice had only drunk two glasses of wine, which she'd ended up paying for herself. She was very aware she hadn't said anything compromising or suggestive, so this could only be another rather dull line of inquiry.

She was pleasantly surprised to be proved wrong.

"About that girl," Dave said, his eyes still fixed on the carpet. "You were asking me about that girl. The one who was on the farm."

Alice waited, and after a pause her patience was rewarded by Dave saying, "I remembered something about her. I'm not sure why now. But I remember her name was Donna. 'Dopey Donna', the kids at the farm used to call her. Kids can be cruel. There was something wrong with her – she was not quite right in the head or something. But I remember talking to her sometimes. I think I was kind to her. I can't quite remember. But I think I brought her sweets back from the village. She liked that. She had a bit of a crush on me. At least, I think she did. Maybe that was someone else. It's all a bit muddled up."

Alice waited expectantly, but there was nothing more to the story. That's all there was. A teenage girl who wasn't quite right in the head who'd had a crush on Dave nearly forty years ago. This time Alice sighed out loud as she headed for the door.

"Go home, Dave. You should take tonight off if you need to. Just call it in early enough so we can get a temporary replacement."

Closing the door behind her, Alice walked down the long corridor in her sensible shoes and sensible twinset to her sensible office, feeling just a little let down that life had never offered her the excitement she secretly craved.

7.

Dave leaned against the window of the bus, watching the rain lash down endlessly. The skies had been so grey for the last couple of days, it was as though all the life and colour had been washed out of the world. The feeling of freedom and possibility he'd felt at the start of the week was gone, replaced by a flat lethargy. He longed to feel that golden glow, that supercharged sense of youth and promise. If he could just recapture it, he might be able to patch things up with Alice and even get her to agree to another date. After all, she had been kind to him these last few days, coming in early just before he finished his shifts and sharing tea and biscuits in the staffroom with him before anyone else arrived. They hadn't talked of much, that was true. Just the awful weather and the TV highlights. But they *had* talked – she wasn't ghosting him after that miserable dinner, and that was something.

If only he could catch that ray of sunshine again with its hope and its summer promise, his life could be so much more than just—

I'm not going near that painting again, he told himself for the hundredth time. *I'm not even going to set foot in the art galleries. Andy can bloody well earn his pay and watch them on the monitors.*

After that last terrible night, his resolve hadn't wavered. For three nights in a row, he'd stayed on the lower floor, doing his rounds of the Egyptian exhibits, the Charles Rennie Mackintosh collection and the wildlife displays without so much as glancing up the stairs. He hadn't even gone near the Poussin exhibition on the lower ground floor. There was something about that shepherdess which unnerved him. Every time he closed his eyes, he saw her face. Except it wasn't *her* face, it was the face of a teenage girl who looked a bit like her, but with frizzy hair instead of curls, and innocent eyes instead of a knowing look. She wasn't pretty, not really. Her nose was too long and she was overweight with crooked teeth, but there was something likeable about her shy, trusting smile when he gave her the sweets he'd bought in the village. He'd promised her more if she'd meet him in the woods that evening, hinting that he might even consider being her boyfriend if she would—

Dave sat up with a jerk. The memory had surfaced from nowhere, diving back into his subconscious before he could grasp it.

Was that Donna I was remembering? he thought to himself, his heart thumping. He knew she'd been at the farm that summer, along with some other teenagers whose faces and names had trickled back to him. But they were all grey and ghostlike, hovering on the edges of his memory like bit players in the wings of a stage. There was a spotlight in his memory, and from time to time, Donna would suddenly appear in it just as the stage went dark and the play ended before he could understand what it had been about.

I was kind to her, though, Dave told himself. *I bought her sweets, didn't I? She liked sweets. That was a kind thing to do.*

But somehow, no matter how many times he told himself that, he couldn't shake the nagging feeling that he wouldn't like the rest of the play if he got the chance to watch to the very end.

He was so busy trying to dredge up submerged memories of the past from his subconscious, he almost missed his stop. Running down the stairs and jumping off at the bridge, he put his umbrella up before crossing the road and hurrying up the Museum steps. He didn't like getting wet. Not after that horrible night when he'd come to his senses in the hallway with Alice looking at him like he'd gone mad. He still wasn't sure what had happened. Perhaps he'd had some kind of mini stroke. He heard people had them all the time without knowing. Maybe that's what had happened. Maybe he should lay off the coffee and stick to Alice's weak tea in future.

He was glad Alice would have left for home long before his shift started this evening. He still hadn't been able to bring himself to take a shower since that horrible scare, and even the feel of water on his skin when he washed his hands was torture. He was starting to smell ripe, despite the layers of deodorant he applied and the fresh underwear he changed into more frequently than usual. At least Andy wouldn't notice. He'd be too busy snoring in front of his monitors.

"Oops, sorry!"

Dave locked the side door behind him, and bumped straight into Holly who had just crossed the hall. A stack of papers a mile high went cascading over the slippery marble, and the trainee curator let out a yelp of distress as she skittered after them in heels that were far too high for Museum work. At least the other young curators had the sense to wear sports shoes, even if they weren't smart enough for Dave's taste.

"Let me, I'll get them." Dave bent down and started gathering up the printouts, feeling his back protesting and silently cursing the young trainee for not doing everything on computer like kids her age were supposed to these days.

"No, no, it's my fault, I should've been looking where I was going." Holly didn't sound like she thought it was her fault, and her knitted brows when Dave finally helped her restack the papers told him she very definitely thought it was him who should've been looking where he was going.

"I wasn't expecting anyone else to be here at this time. Apart from Betty and Jim in the staffroom, of course. They'll be handing over to me from the day shift."

"Yes, I saw them down there," Holly said, a trace of irritation in her voice as she stood up again, balancing the sheets in a precarious pile in her arms. "I was working late. I've been chasing some interesting research leads. There's only one permanent position coming up, and three of us are interning here, so it's all getting a bit competitive."

Dave wasn't quite sure what 'interning' was – it sounded vaguely like a funeral term to him – but he didn't ask. He said instead, "Aren't you at least going to put your notes in a bag? You'll get them soaked before you're halfway to the bus stop."

Holly looked at him like he was mad. "My car's just there." She nodded out of the glass-panelled door at the shiny red Hyundai parked near the entrance steps. "What kind of idiot gets the bus in weather like this?" Noticing too late the tell-tale spots of rain on Dave's jacket, she bit her lip and hurried to the door, looking even more shame-faced when she realised she didn't have a free hand to get her keys and Dave had to unlock it again for her.

"Have a good night," she called over her shoulder as she clacked down the steps in her heels.

"Yeah, you too," Dave called as cheerfully as he could. His heart sank further as he relocked the door, watching her drive away in the expensive car that her parents must've bought for her, or else the kids her age working in the Museum were getting paid a salary he could only dream of. It felt like yet another reminder that he was a middle-aged man whose youth was gone and who'd spent his whole life working for minimum wage with nothing to show for it.

The handover from the day-shift team didn't lift his spirits any. Betty was showing off photos of her grandkids, and Jim was on his last shift before he took three weeks off to visit his brother in Australia, courtesy of his sister-in-law's family who owned a vineyard in the Adelaide Hills. Even Andy seemed to be in a chirpy mood as he sat down at the monitors, buoyed up by the prospect of his daughter's wedding in the coming weeks.

Everyone seemed to have a life outside work, and their job was merely the superficial paid time that marked the transition from one more meaningful experience to the next. All Dave had was his job. He didn't even have a dog or a cat who would mourn his passing if he fell under the bus at the end of yet another shift.

When the hell did I get this morbid? he wondered, waving Betty and Jim off and wishing he had somewhere better to be, too. *I used to like working here. I used to be content.*

It was all that damn painting's fault. Ever since he'd seen it, he'd been troubled by the nagging thought that there was once a time, long ago, when anything seemed possible, and that his life held endless promise. If only his parents hadn't got divorced, then maybe he'd—

No, that wasn't it. Half the people he worked with had divorced parents. They hadn't let life pass them by as a consequence. It must've been more than that. There must be something holding him back, some force at work against him, miring his life in the boggy ground of mundanity that he'd never been able to escape from.

Maybe he should ask Alice out again. She'd been nice to him all week, she wasn't avoiding him. Maybe if he tried a little harder he could kindle some small spark there that might, in time, burn a little brighter than the flicker of interest he currently felt for her.

If only he had the courage to try again. If only he could recapture that feeling of hope and invincibility he'd had when he was sixteen. If only—

Without realising it, Dave found his circuit of the museum had wound him up the stairs and around the galleries to the Scottish art room.

I'll just take a look, he told himself. *I won't touch it this time. It can't hurt me if I just look.*

The glowing golden colours of sunlight on mountains and meadow grass and the riot of wild flowers seemed more vivid than ever. Dave felt the restless tension build up inside him as he stared at the painting, a yearning for the past so deep it ached.

I wish I could have frozen time that summer, Dave sighed to himself, even though he could barely remember a single moment of his stay on the farm. All he had were flashes of intense memory, so bright they almost dazzled him.

A feeling of purpose as he strode about from chore to chore, sunlight on his neck as he painted fences and mucked out barns.

A feeling of wellbeing as he sat down to a well-earned dinner, an inviting bed waiting for him each evening.

Laughter with the other teenagers as they ran down

the hill together in the golden glow of youth, racing each other back to the farmhouse before the sun could set and stars came out in the vast expanse of Highland sky.

There had been so much to look forward to back then, so much to hope for, so much—

Dave couldn't help it. The yearning inside himself was too strong. His hand reached out, trying to catch at the golden light of youth that glimmered just beyond his reach.

There was a fizz of pain and a blinding flash, and next moment he was back in the meadow, the weight of years falling from his shoulders and the sweet scent of summer grass filling his lungs with fresh vitality. He felt rejuvenated, reborn. There was nothing he couldn't do, the future was wide open and waiting, everything still to play for.

I'll just stay a few moments, he told himself, making sure the bright patch of sunlight slowly tracing a path across the meadow was within easy reach. *Just long enough to catch my breath and take this feeling home with me for good. Then I'll go straight to the phone and ask Alice if she wants to go away for the weekend. To hell with the rent and the bills. I'll hire a little self-catering cottage in the countryside and we can get to know each other properly. Make up for lost time.*

So much lost time.

He could picture it all now – a cosy little getaway somewhere amongst rolling hills where they could go for long walks in the woods and meadows. Somewhere like this. Perhaps if it was still standing, he'd even be able to rent this very—

A door slammed in the distance.

Dave jumped, whirling round.

Someone was coming out of the farmhouse. A figure walked down the path, heading straight across the meadow towards him.

The light was fading fast in the east, the figure's face hidden in shadow. Dave felt the cold hand of foreboding clutch at his heart as he watched the figure draw nearer. He recognised the shambling gait. A memory surfaced again briefly – a girl with frizzy hair and trusting eyes, her footsteps not quite steady. She'd been eighteen, but seemed younger, her innocent smile widening at the promise of more sweets to come if she would meet in the woods after sundown, when everyone else was in bed.

Meet who? Dave wondered, seeing the figure veer off, skirting the pond to the far bank at the edge of the woods.

His question was soon answered. He didn't hear the farmhouse door slam this time, but something made him turn around again and look over his shoulder. The light on this side of the meadow was vanishing, almost as though a painter had loaded a brush with black ink and was smearing it across a canvas.

It was the second figure who was sucking the light from the painting. A sinister force seemed to be emanating from him, a pulsing, malevolent intent that coalesced like dark matter around him.

Him? Yes, Dave knew the second figure was male with just as much certainty as he knew the first figure had been Donna. The memories crept up on him, smuggled back under cover of darkness. He watched, rooted helplessly to the spot as the second figure skirted the edge of the pond too, the light around him swallowed up, leaving only empty black space behind him.

The first figure was shivering. The sun was setting and she was getting cold. She hadn't brought a jacket. She hadn't really thought this through. She didn't want to be out after sundown, she just wanted the packet of jelly babies she'd been promised. She didn't understand what it was she'd agreed to.

Dave knew. A growing sense of dread filled him as he watched the second figure near the shivering girl, the world behind him blotted out with black ink with each footstep he took towards her.

Run! he wanted to yell at the girl, but his throat was dry and his tongue felt as though it was stuck to the roof his mouth.

The second figure reached out, pulling the girl roughly towards him. She didn't resist at first, unsure what was happening. He'd always been so nice to her before, saying kind words and buying her sweets while the other teenagers just laughed at her. But he wasn't being kind this time, and his hands were poking and prodding in places she didn't like, and his words were harsh and the things he was doing hurt and she didn't want the jelly babies that much after all, and—

Dave watched the girl struggle up, stumbling at the edge of the pond as she tried to get away.

Let her go! Dave pleaded, watching the second figure grab her arm again, tendrils of black ink wrapping her limbs in shadow. *She won't tell, she's too frightened. Just let her go before it's too late.*

It was already too late. As the figures struggled by the water's edge, Dave knew with sickening inevitability what would happen next. The girl wasn't steady on her feet. One more pawing hand grabbing at her was all it took to topple her over as she fought desperately to escape. There was a soft splash as she hit the water, not the loud crash that Dave was sure he remembered.

The second figure stood frozen for a long moment, watching the girl struggle and splutter in the murky pond.

Why don't you help her? Dave yelled inside his own mind, the words refusing to sound out loud. *Why don't you pull her out?*

He knew why.

He hadn't realised the pond had been so deep. He thought she was playing for sympathy and attention. He hadn't known her feet really couldn't touch the bottom until it was too late.

By the time the second figure jumped into the water, it was already futile. The first figure had vanished. Darkness settled like a black cloud over the pond as the second figure surfaced again, his arms empty.

Go and get help! Wake people up! Call the police! Dave thought. But the darkness merely intensified as the second figure pulled himself back onto the bank and vanished into the pitch-black half of the tainted painting he'd destroyed.

Dave knew where he was going. Not to the front door and the phone. There was a tall coal shed below the windows at the back of the farmhouse. Standing on the roof, a teenage boy could just manage to pull himself up to the bedroom window above. A quick change of clothes and straight to bed, and then no one would ever know. Not until the woods had been searched for days and the pond had been dredged.

It didn't matter that questions would be asked. The deed would be wiped from his memory the same way that half of the painting had been plunged into darkness.

But it wasn't half of the painting. It was more than half. The edge of the black curtain was creeping forward as something clawed its way out of the pond and came twitching and jerking across the grass on all fours towards Dave. He could feel its malign intent. It wanted to reach him before he could escape. It wanted to make him *pay.*

I'm sorry, Donna, Dave thought, his heart aching with guilt and grief. *I'm so, so sorry. But I don't belong here in the past with you and these memories. I have to go home.*

He turned to race back to the patch of light that was his link to the world of the present, the slowly sinking life raft that would carry him to safety.

But not this time.

The sunlit spot was gone.

He'd stayed too long in the painting, and the sun had set behind the mountain peaks.

Dave whirled around, searching for an escape route, but there was nowhere to go. Darkness was closing in on all sides now, the final curtain drawn by the figure twitching towards him. He forced his feet to move, to run into the darkness – anywhere – to escape the grasping arms covered in pondweed and stinking of death.

But it was too late – forty years too late.

Slithering, eel-like fingers grasped his leg, pulling

him off balance and tugging him back over boggy ground to the edge of the pond.

"No! I'm sorry! I'm sorry!" Dave sobbed, trying to grasp at tufts of grass and patches of bushy heather, but they were all gone, sinking into the black mire as the darkness blotted out everything good that had once been in the sunlit painting. His legs were dragged into ice-cold pond water, weeds tangling around his feet and pulling him deeper and deeper.

One last gasp was all that Dave got before the water closed over his head and darkness rushed down his throat, drowning his final scream.

8.

"Holly, calm down! For goodness' sake, pull yourself together!"

Alice was an hour and a half early for work, and she hadn't even had time for a cup of tea yet, never mind a slice of toast and a biscuit. She was in no mood to humour the young trainee curator's attempts to get her attention at this time of the morning. Holly was keen and fairly competent, but if she thought her chances of being taken on permanently would be improved by ruining Alice's morning routine, she was dead wrong.

Alice wasn't a people person. She liked to come in

early so she could have peace and quiet to work before her colleagues and the annoying Museum visitors cluttered up the place. The last way she wanted to start the day was with a half-hysterical intern having what looked suspiciously like a panic attack in the entrance hall when she was barely in the door herself.

"But I don't understand how it happened!" Holly was gibbering. "It wasn't my fault, I've only just come in and seen it!"

"Seen what?" Alice shook out her umbrella and placed it in the coat stand as usual, refusing to be distracted from her morning routine.

"The painting! It's been completely destroyed!"

Alice felt her heart almost stop in her chest, and her hand flew to her mouth. "Not the Poussin!" she gasped. "Please don't say—"

"No, that exhibition's fine, it was the first thing I checked. I mean upstairs – the new painting. Come and see!"

Her morning routine well and truly ruined now, Alice abandoned her coat on the front desk and went hurrying up the stairs behind the young intern. She had no idea what to expect. A day-time attack could mean a slashed canvas, a pot of paint thrown at a painting or even a can of beans poured onto a work of art as a form of political protest. But a painting destroyed overnight? How could anyone have got in and out without being seen?

She raced down the long gallery to the Scottish section, skidding to a stop in her sensible shoes before the Museum's latest acquisition. She couldn't quite believe what she was seeing. How could that even..?

"Quick, help me get it off the wall," she barked, instantly snapping into preservation mode. "We need to make sure the other paintings aren't at risk."

But when, between the two of them, they managed to unhook the painting and set it on the floor, Alice blinked, utterly confused. She reached out to touch the wall behind, running her hand across the plaster to make sure.

"I don't understand it!" she murmured, half to herself.

"That's what I've been saying!" Holly put in, earning herself even more negative Brownie points for playing the 'I told you so' card.

"Get Dave and Andy up here," Alice commanded, making sure the young intern knew who was boss. "They must have seen something."

"Andy's on his way, and I already called the Director. She's stuck in traffic, but she'll be here soon."

"Hmph," was all Alice said in reply. Maybe the young intern wasn't so bad after all. At least she'd kept her head and followed procedure.

"I was up late last night doing some research," Holly

started, hoping to break the uncomfortable silence as they waited. "And I think I've tracked down the painting's location."

"Oh?" Alice glanced up, interested.

"It's a farm in the Cairngorms – it was owned by the elderly man who made the bequest. I think it was his family farm, but they sold up and moved away in the nineteen seventies, and they've lived in Glasgow ever since."

"Financial troubles?" Alice asked. Her young intern was definitely proving more promising by the minute.

"No, a family tragedy – a drowning, I think, going by the news reports. They lost a daughter. Didn't want to stay after that. I think they ran a summer camp for teenagers, and one year—"

She was interrupted by the heavy tread of someone out of shape who was jogging along the gallery, and a moment later Andy came wheezing in to join them. The sleepy glaze had gone from his eyes, and he looked more alert than Alice had ever seen him. The thought of his job being on the line over this had obviously lit a fire under him.

"Well?" Alice demanded, pointing down at the painting on the floor.

"It's been quiet all night!" Andy protested, having clearly rehearsed his speech on the way upstairs. "No one's been in or out all night except me and Dave, until

Holly came in this morning. I reviewed the footage, but the camera on this floor went out about half two, so we haven't got anything except static on file."

"You didn't think to come up and check when the camera feed suddenly went dark?" Alice asked, a dangerous edge to her usually calm voice.

"Dave was walking up the stairs at the time. If there was anything going on up here, he'd have radioed down to let me know. I didn't think anything of it," Andy muttered defensively.

"Where *is* Dave?" Holly asked, looking round. "He isn't answering his phone. I thought he was downstairs with you. He's not in the staffroom – that's where I went to store my coat when I first came in. Have you seen him?"

"Not since I saw him coming up here on the monitor," Andy admitted. "He's been acting a bit funny lately," he added quickly, keen to lay the blame for the security lapse elsewhere. "I didn't want to mention it, but a couple of times this week, I've seen him come in here and…" he trailed off, biting his lip as though thinking better of being disloyal.

"And what?" Alice said icily, making it clear that there was a job on the line, and Andy better make sure it wasn't his.

"Well, the way the camera's angled, I could see into this room – just this side, mind," he said reluctantly, pointing at the wall where they'd just removed the artwork. "He'd stand looking at that painting for hours, like he couldn't take his eyes off it. If that was all, it would be bad enough, but..." he hesitated again, struggling with his conscience.

Alice waited. She knew Andy wasn't going to jump under the bus if there was someone else he could throw there in his place.

"Dave's a good bloke, a solid security officer, he should know better than to do what he did," Andy said at last.

"And what did he do?" Alice sounded like she was going to start pulling out instruments of torture if Andy didn't get to the point soon.

"He *touched* the painting," Andy said slowly, like he almost couldn't believe it himself. "He'd put his hand on it, and stand there for *hours*. I know I should've said something, but come on, this is *Dave* we're talking about. I was going to have a quiet word with him about it last night, but…"

"But you fell asleep and only woke up when Holly called you this morning?" Alice finished for him.

Andy stared shame-faced at his shoes.

"I don't get it," Holly said slowly. "I know touching the artwork's a sackable offence, I mean, he could've left sweat on the surface that might've stained over time, but this? How the hell could he have done *this* to an oil painting without getting the wall or the floor wet?"

Andy frowned. He hadn't actually seen what the damage was. He'd only heard Holly shouting down the phone at him that a painting had been destroyed, and he'd scrambled to review the footage straight away. Now, when he stepped around Alice to take a look, he let out an audible gasp.

The landscape painting was unrecognisable. Long streaks of some kind of liquid had washed the colours away, as though the painting had been hung under a waterfall. There was nothing left of the original scene, save for a dark patch of congealed paint where once there had been a pond. Andy gazed open-mouthed at the water-damaged painting, then back at the space on the wall where it had once hung.

The plaster behind was bone dry, not a hint of damp to suggest the painting had ever been hung in anything other than perfect conditions.

Andy stared at the painting again. There was something about that dark patch of paint that made him shudder. Just for a moment, he thought he caught a glimpse of a face staring out at him in a silent scream. He jumped back as though he'd been burned, his heart hammering in fright.

"I'm going to make a pot of coffee," he muttered, hurrying for the stairs. "The Director can sort this out with Dave when she gets here, if she can find him. It was his job to patrol up here, not mine. I just watch the monitors, and I didn't see anything."

He took the stairs to the lower floor two at a time, the hair on the back of his neck prickling eerily the whole way down.

ET IN ARCADIA EGO

The Shape of the Beast

1.

It was the same argument they'd been having every day this week, and Thelma was getting sick of it. She was determined not to lose this time. Just because she was a cleaner and Holly was a curator-in-training, it didn't give the jumped-up little intern the right to boss her about.

"My hours are five to eight p.m.," Thelma said, brandishing the hose of her vacuum cleaner at the group crowding around the taxidermy cases of the Museum's natural history section. "I have the same routine every day. The Director hasn't told me to skip work to fit in with your last-minute plans. This is the room I always clean at this time, so unless I hear otherwise from the boss, this is the room I'm cleaning now."

"I'm not asking you to skip work!" Holly shouted over the whine of the vacuum cleaner. "I'm just asking you to use your mop while I give my talk in here. There isn't even any carpet to hoover, it's just laminated floorboards!"

Thelma noted with satisfaction that the young intern was growing hoarse. A week of arguing over the same thing would do that to an over-zealous little tyrant who thought she had the right to order the lesser-paid staff around. Filing the fact that Holly was only an intern currently living off a small Museum grant under 'things that aren't relevant to my argument', Thelma pressed home her advantage, which was her louder, more strident voice.

"I need to use the vacuum cleaner to suck the dust out of the hard-to-reach places," she bellowed over the loud droning that, if she was being honest, was starting to give her a headache. "You'd know that if you actually had to do some real work around here instead of—"

Just as she was about to win her argument, the vacuum cleaner made a strange noise that sounded like a strangled cough, before cutting out. In the silence that followed, Thelma could hear some of the students in the group sighing with relief.

Little shits, she thought resentfully. *Just wait till you're out in the real world and have to make a living instead of dossing about at university.*

Not that any of the group of international students would ever know what trying to make ends meet on minimum wage would be like. They were cherry-picked master's degree students on a week-long residential course at the university on the other side of the park. They'd been given after-hours access to the exhibits to fit in with their daytime lecture schedule, and Holly had managed to ensure their guided tours had clashed with Thelma's cleaning routine every day since Monday.

"Well, that seems to have decided things," Holly said, clearing her aching throat with a little too much satisfaction for Thelma's liking. "Now, group, where were we..?"

Thelma gave the mutinous vacuum cleaner a sharp kick as Holly went back to her history of the Museum's taxidermy exhibits. It didn't help. All it achieved was to loosen the sole of Thelma's shoe that she'd already glued back in place twice this month. Shoes were a terrible price these days. Even the charity shops seemed to have forgotten they were selling second-hand goods and were pricing their donated clothes as if they were flogging celebrity cast-offs.

It's all these bloody middle-class students thinking 'second hand' is a trendy way to virtue signal, and pricing those of us who need cheap clothes out of the market, Thelma thought angrily, giving up on the vacuum cleaner and turning to her mop and bucket instead. Sloshing her mop around the laminated floorboards didn't make nearly as much noise as she would've liked, but at least she had the satisfaction of getting water all over the students' expensive trainers as they stood around listening to Holly's talk.

"...and this female black bear has been in the Museum's collection for over a hundred years. It was donated by a Russian naturalist who brought it over from Southern Siberia when he emigrated here in the early nineteen hundreds. It's one of the best-preserved specimens in the country – most examples of taxidermy begin to deteriorate after—"

"I don't agree with the killing of the animals and making them to be things on display," a student with a heavy German accent interrupted. "I think that is wrong."

Several other students nodded in agreement. Holly gave them all an indulgent smile, clearly used to answering the same objection on these tours.

"The Museum's policy is not to acquire new taxidermy specimens, but to maintain the ones gifted to our collections in the past for their historical value," she said smoothly. "After consultation with the general public and other stake holders, we've sold our butterfly exhibits and replaced them with video displays, and we no longer have a permanent display of live bees or beetles. We do take the issue of animal welfare very seriously at this Museum, I can assure you of that." Holly flicked her blonde ponytail back over her shoulder and tried to change the subject just as quickly. "Now, if you'll follow me to the fossil exhibits, you'll see some—"

"I don't think it is right," the German student interrupted loudly again. "I don't think dead animals should be put in glass boxes for people to stare at."

Thelma grinned to herself, rewarding the obnoxious student by not drowning his shoes. She moved her mop around the back of the group instead, eager to hear how the smug little intern was going to deal with this one.

"Yes, it is a contentious issue, and there are a number of differing views on the subject," Holly replied, an edge of exasperation to her bright smile. "Now, as time is getting on, if we could—"

"What is that?"

It was a French student who'd interrupted this time. She was peering into the glass case, frowning at a large lump of what looked like play-doh beside the black bear. She pushed her spectacles right up her nose, but she seemed to be struggling to read the small print on the sign next to the exhibit.

"Oh, that was something one of the previous interns put there as part of his final project presentation," Holly said, glancing at the German student and deciding an explanation would only provoke him further. "It should have been taken down ages ago, so thanks for reminding me. Now, if we could—"

"Yes, but what *is* it?"

Thelma didn't bother to hide her loud snigger. She

might not have won the argument over the vacuuming, but the insufferable students were more than making up for it. She leaned on her mop and raised an eyebrow at Holly, letting her know she was enjoying watching her squirm.

Holly scowled back, deciding the best course of action was to resort to full-scale lecture mode to drown the students out. "It's an artistic depiction of a medieval legend regarding bears," she told the group, raising her strained voice to make it clear she would brook no interruptions this time. "According to folk tales, since bears give birth in the depths of winter, cubs are born as shapeless lumps of eyeless flesh. It's the job of the mother bear to shape them into their proper form by licking them when they're born. That's where the term 'to lick into shape' comes from, for those of you who like English idioms," she added.

Some of the students nodded, while others, with more limited English, simply looked blank.

"It's thought the idea was a corruption of the church's doctrine that humans are born imperfect, deformed by original sin, and need to be shaped by the tongue of the church's teaching. The last intern was doing a doctoral thesis on the intersection of religion and civic institutions, with a focus on sacred objects in secular museums."

Sounds like a complete bloody waste of time and

taxpayers' money, Thelma thought to herself, going back to sloshing water around the floor to make it clear it was time for the students to move on. The French student still didn't get the hint despite the small lake forming around her sports shoes.

"Yes, but why is the sign with *this* bear, and not on a display board?"

The French student's English was much better than the German student's – she wasn't going to be put off so easily by Holly's fast-paced delivery.

Holly looked uncomfortable again, and Thelma saw with relish that she'd been hiding something that would make the rest of her tour extremely awkward.

"Well, it was thought that if a mother bear was killed before her malformed cubs could be licked into shape, then they became demons who exacted their revenge on sinful humans," she said as quickly as she could as though hoping most of the international students wouldn't be able to follow her words. "It was noted in the specimen files that this bear was pregnant when it was shot, so that's where the intern must have got the idea from. Anyway, we really do have to—"

A chorus of protests drowned out her words. Holly had been wrong. A number of the students had an almost perfect grasp of English, and those who didn't, like the German student, were smart enough to go along with the crowd when they sensed controversy brewing.

"Right, we'll move on to the fossils – you can leave all comments and suggestions on today's evaluation forms," Holly shouted over the noise, marching on to the next room with a cheery grin fixed desperately to her face.

Thelma laughed to herself as the students filed out behind her, grumbling to each other in various languages. *Serves her bloody right,* she thought gleefully. *Teach her not to be so damn up herself next time. Thanks, little blob.* She tapped the glass where the formless lump of modelling clay lay in the cabinet between the paws of the mother bear.

Humming to herself, Thelma finished her work in the taxidermy room, not even minding now that the water she'd carelessly sloshed around was soaking her tights through the broken sole of her shoe and that she'd have to tie it up with elastic bands for the long walk home.

She didn't often come out on top with people who were richer or better educated.

Today had been a good day.

2.

"Thanks, Thelma, you're such a sweetheart. What would

I do without you?"

Rachel leaned back on the pillows Thelma had plumped up for her and took a sip of the tea she'd been brought.

"It's no bother, I'm happy to do it," Thelma smiled, moving the tray of biscuits on the bedside table closer so Rachel could reach them. *Though I'd be a bit happier if you paid me more*, she added to herself.

She shouldn't grumble. Rachel had heard a year ago that her former classmate was having financial difficulties, and had offered her the cleaning job to help Thelma out. It wasn't Rachel's fault that she'd been born pretty and had the kind of golden charm that seemed to bring nothing but good fortune her way. It wasn't Rachel's fault that their lives had turned out so differently.

Thelma turned away and began putting the clothes she'd ironed into the wardrobe. She tried hard not to let the resentment get the better of her, but… God, it was hard not to feel bitter about how much luckier Rachel had been in life. Thelma could remember right back to that first day of school, when she'd been dumped at the school gate in second-hand clothes and tangled hair by her overworked single mother, while Rachel had skipped in holding her own beautiful mother's hand, her shoes polished, her new uniform neatly pressed and her luxuriant black hair carefully braided into plaits.

Teachers were supposed to treat pupils all the same, but Thelma had learned early on that children who were smart, pretty, or rich got preferential treatment. All the way through school, Rachel was praised for her sunny outlook on life and cheerful personality. By the time they started secondary school, her angelic smile had become her trademark, while Thelma's awkwardness and nervous frown seemed to instantly antagonise her teachers and her classmates alike.

"Stop mumbling, why can't you speak up like Rachel?" her teachers would snap at her when she was called on to answer a question she inevitably got wrong. *"You make people uncomfortable by being so nervous,"* one teacher had said accusingly when she'd stared red-faced at the desk, barely holding back tears as she listened to another tirade about her failings. *"If you just smiled like Rachel does, you'd get on with people a lot better."*

It's easy for some people to smile through life, Thelma thought resentfully. *If you have a loving family with money and no problems, people treat you differently right from the start. You learn that people want to be your friend, that you're valuable. Boys want to date you and teachers give you all the help you need to do well in exams. Not like me. No one wanted to help me, even when I was five years old and clearly in need of a hot meal and adult attention. No teachers ever explained anything to me. No one wanted to be my friend. No boys ever wanted to date me.*

It was no wonder that Rachel – with her charming, sunny smile – had gone on to university to become a teacher, marrying a doctor and moving to a lovely house in the city's West End with rose gardens and posh cafes and holidays in the Mediterranean every year.

Thelma had struggled and failed to pass any of her exams, held back by her shyness in school and her chaotic home life. Now she lived in a council flat in the worst part of the city, with neighbours who made noise at all hours of the night and day, and worse, she'd never been asked out in her whole life. She'd had the same dreams as Rachel – a career, a husband, a nice house. But none of her dreams had come true. And all because of the bad luck of birth that had piled troubles and worries on her from a young age while Rachel had the perfect start that helped her to smile warmly at everyone.

Well, Rachel wasn't smiling now. Not since she lost the baby a few weeks ago.

Thelma glanced back at Rachel in the wardrobe mirror. Without makeup, her face was paler than it used to be, but she was still every bit as pretty as she'd always been. She looked far younger than her thirty-eight years. Thelma, on the other hand, was often mistaken for a woman in her early fifties. Her face was lined with care, and her brown hair was peppered with grey. She couldn't afford to dye it regularly, not on her low wages, and her clothes were cheap and dowdy. Rachel had kindly offered to give her some of her own clothes when she was pregnant and had a wardrobe clear-out, but Thelma would never have been able to fit her flabby belly and saggy chest into the svelte dresses and skirts that Rachel wore.

Rachel was always doing kind things like that. It made Thelma so mad she wanted to spit in Rachel's face.

You've always thought you were so much better than me, haven't you? Thelma thought, glaring at Rachel in the mirror. *Your mother was always acting so concerned, making a big show of giving me your cast-off shoes that everyone laughed at in class, and telling all the mothers at the school gate that she needed to walk me home as there was no one to 'look after me'. She loved pretending to care to show everyone how 'kind' she was, and you're just the same. So bloody virtuous. It makes me sick.*

"I've got to get on now – my cleaning shift starts in an hour and it's a bit of a walk to the Museum," Thelma said, closing the wardrobe door and picking up the laundry basket.

"Oh, can I lend you the bus fare? It's an awfully long way to go in those shoes." Rachel looked with concern at the shoe Thelma had spent the better part of an hour gluing back together the night before.

Thelma bit back a nasty reply. *All this bloody wealth*, she thought, glancing around the tastefully decorated bedroom, *and you offer to lend me money instead of offering to raise my slave wages.*

"It's fine, thanks. I'm used to it."

"Well, I suppose it's good exercise, and it's cheaper than a gym membership, isn't it?" Rachel smiled at her, a weaker version of the charming smile she'd always worn before she lost her baby. It was a pale imitation, but it was enough to enrage Thelma.

"I wouldn't know how much a gym membership costs," she muttered. "Can I get you anything else before I go?"

"Nothing, thanks, you've been such a help this afternoon," Rachel said, the ghost of her former smile still on her lips. "I'll be back on my feet any day now, and then I'll be able to make my own tea and biscuits and you won't have to do so much running after me."

"It's no trouble," Thelma lied, kicking herself for doing what everyone always did. Pandering to Rachel. Pampering her. Treating her like a little princess. And all because she was pretty and had a nice smile.

Don't get smug again, Rachel Benson, Thelma thought

to herself as she stomped down the stairs. *I took that smile from you once, and I can do it again if you get too big for your boots.*

3.

When Thelma wheeled her mop and bucket into the taxidermy room, she found it wasn't just the international students who were missing that evening. The large blob of black clay at the foot of the stuffed bear was gone too, along with the small hand-written sign the previous intern had left beside it.

Pity, Thelma thought. *I liked watching that young intern squirm when it was mentioned. I could've used it another time if she got in my way in here.*

For all Thelma disliked the other Museum staff and the way they looked down at her, she was sorry to see the group of international students go. Arguing with Holly had been the highlight of her week – a rare opportunity for human contact. Before her miscarriage, Rachel had often been marking schoolwork in her study when Thelma came to clean. And although she hadn't been working for the last couple of weeks, Rachel had mostly been tired and sleeping when Thelma visited before her Museum shift. She hardly ever saw Rachel's doctor husband, but what she had seen of him – all confident ease and suave charm – had made her envy Rachel even more. Thelma knew she could never attract a man like that. Even Dave, the Museum security guard who used to work the night shift, had never given her so much as a second glance, and he'd been nearly fifteen years older, sixty pounds overweight and going bald.

Thelma hated the silence of the Museum after hours. With the curators and interns working down in their offices and storage rooms, and the security guards spending the first half of their shift in the CCTV room, Thelma was on her own up here on the ground floor. There was usually a team of four cleaners, but the others were all out on strike just now. Thelma couldn't afford to be part of a union and risk losing what little job security she had. Besides, the other cleaners all had husbands and second incomes as backup if they lost their jobs. All Thelma had to rely on was herself and her own hard graft.

It wasn't just the sound of human chatter that Thelma missed. Annoying though the gossip of the other cleaners could be, it masked the sound that seemed to echo through the silence when Thelma was on her own. She could almost hear the ticking of her biological clock echoing down the corridors of the empty Museum every time she worked on her own. It was one of the reasons she insisted on dragging her old vacuum cleaner around with her despite the complete absence of carpets everywhere except the offices. The slosh of her mop and bucket couldn't drown out the sound that seemed to thud in her ears with each beat of her heart.

Tick. Tick. Tick, the noise went. *You're running out of time. Tock. Tock. Tock.*

Thelma had always wanted children. She'd longed for them ever since she was a small child, lovingly carrying the one-armed doll around that her mother scrounged from a jumble-sale bin, and pretending it was her very own living, breathing baby. She'd cried for a month when her mother had thrown it out when she was seven, telling Thelma she was too old for toys and needed to grow the hell up. If any of the boys at secondary school had so much as looked twice at Thelma, she would've had a baby with them in a heartbeat, consequences be damned. But her mother couldn't afford the electricity to run a washing machine, and there was no heating to dry clothes on a radiator. Thelma's smelly uniform coupled with terrible luck in the looks department had made her a pariah, and even the most desperate teenage boys had considered her beneath their notice.

She'd once heard a group of sixteen-year-old boys sniggering that she was a 'two bagger'. She hadn't understood what it meant until one of the unkind girls in her class had taken great delight in informing Thelma she'd need to wear a bag over her head for anyone to consider sleeping with her, and that she was so ugly a boy would need to wear a second one himself in case hers fell off. Rachel had jumped in and told the girl to stop being so cruel. Her face had been so pious as she told the other girls that they shouldn't pick on those less fortunate than themselves, that Thelma had fought the urge to slap her.

Well, I got my own back eventually, didn't I? Thelma thought to herself as she dragged her mop around the varnished floorboards angrily. *She's learned what tough luck is, and she's learned it's not so easy to smile when bad things happen and your life's not all golden sunshine.*

Still, what Thelma had done didn't quite sit right. She hadn't meant to do Rachel any real harm. Just a few weeks of bad morning sickness, that's all the daily powder in her cup was meant to cause. Thelma had enjoyed offering Rachel tea as she worked on her computer after school while Thelma had cleaned her house and cooked dinner for her husband coming home. She liked the feeling of power it gave her, opening those packets and slipping the contents inside, then watching out of the corner of her eye as Rachel sipped the brew. She wouldn't have done it if Rachel had just had a normal pregnancy like everyone else, with dark circles under her eyes from lack of sleep and a queasy look on her face from vomiting all through the first trimester. But of course, she hadn't. Like everything else, Rachel's pregnancy had been golden, and she'd been so healthy she was practically glowing by the five-month mark.

Thelma simply couldn't bear it. Rachel had everything – a golden life and a golden job with the promise of a golden pension and a golden house and a golden husband, and finally she had the very thing that Thelma longed for more than anything: a baby. And even that had been perfect and golden too.

Right up until the moment Thelma took it from her.

I didn't mean it, Thelma told herself again, repeating the words stubbornly and refusing to give in to the nagging voice that told her she should feel guilty. *Those doses were just meant to make her vomit for a few weeks, nothing more. It's not my fault if I didn't mean it, is it?*

Running her mop along the bottom of one of the display cases, she glanced up to see the glass eyes of the black bear staring back at her accusingly.

"What are you looking at?" Thelma muttered. "You don't know anything about it."

The after-hours lights in the room were lower than the usual daytime ones, but they still glinted faintly off the glass, their small circles glowing along the length of the display case. Out of the corner of her eye, Thelma saw the shadow of something moving behind one of those yellow circles.

There was something in the display case, something that seemed to be crawling between the paws of the black bear.

Thelma peered into the case, but on closer inspection, there was nothing else there, just the black bear staring dead-eyed back at her.

Must be tired, Thelma thought. *No bloody wonder. I work my fingers to the bone for practically no money, and—*

The shadow moved again. This time it wasn't behind the circle of light, but superimposed on top – a reflection on the glass.

Which meant there was something outside the case. Something behind her.

Thelma whirled round, but there was nothing there. The opposite wall was blank, a simple sign announcing the Museum was awaiting the arrival of a new display.

Christ, I don't get paid enough to work in a place infested with rats! Thelma thought to herself as she dumped her mop back in her bucket and headed for the stairs. *Maybe I should've joined that damn union after all. At least I'd have people to talk to if I was on the picket lines and I wouldn't be going half barmy being on my own so much.*

4.

"It's really kind of you to come here with me, Thelma," Rachel said, brushing away the tear that was threatening to spoil her perfect makeup. "Gerald doesn't like visiting Jonathan – it's still too raw for him just yet."

"It's no trouble," Thelma said through gritted teeth. "I'm happy to help. Whatever you need."

Her fingers tightened around the bunch of flowers she'd been handed as Rachel bent down to lay the stuffed bear on the gravestone. This was the last place she wanted to be, but she needed the money Rachel paid her, and when Rachel asked Thelma to accompany her to the cemetery today rather than clean her house, Thelma couldn't think of a way to say no.

You only want me here because you don't want that smiley mask to slip in front of your fancy friends, she thought angrily. *You can't bear to show the world anything other than a perfect version of your life. That's why you only invited your immediate family to the funeral instead of your friends and work colleagues. And me, of course. You needed someone to prepare the buffet and hand round drinks at your perfect after-ceremony reception.*

Thelma knew that wasn't fair. But she had to tell

herself that Rachel wasn't really hurt, that her show of grief was just an act. Believing otherwise would open Thelma up to a whole world of guilt that she wasn't prepared to own.

"Jonathan was too good for this world," Rachel sighed. "Maybe that's why God took him so early."

Christ, it wasn't even old enough to be viable and you went and named it, Thelma scowled to herself. *And of course that baby was golden. Just like everything else in your life. You would've been an absolutely insufferable mother, just like your own was,* she thought, remembering all the times Rachel's mother had made a show of patronising her and giving her charity handouts in front of the other parents. *Maybe I did the world a favour.*

Thelma tasted the bitterness behind the evil words swirling in her head as she swallowed them down, handing Rachel a tissue and placing the flowers on the grave in a small act of contrition. This hadn't been what she wanted, but now that it had happened, she had to pretend to herself it was all for the best, or the guilt would never allow her another good night's sleep again.

"It's so peaceful here, isn't it?" Rachel sighed, looking over at the small copse of trees that bordered the cemetery. "I like to think of him being somewhere quiet and pretty."

Wiping her eyes for a final time with the edge of her

tissue, Rachel turned away and began heading back up the path to her car. Thelma was just about to follow, when she saw something darting between the trees beyond the last line of headstones. For a moment, she thought it might have been a fox. It was too big for a rabbit, and she didn't think there were badgers on the outskirts of the city.

But the shapes of those animals would all have been recognisable. This thing – this *shadow* – was formless, a misshapen mass that moved on no legs and stared back at her with no eyes from a head that wasn't really a head at all, just—

Thelma clutched her handbag to her chest and hurried after Rachel.

Even nature's on her side, Thelma thought sourly. *She gets to feel calm and at rest here, and all I get is nature making me feel like I don't belong and I'm not welcome here. Someone up there's been having a bloody good laugh at my expense ever since I was born.*

She glared up at the sky that had soaked her on her walk to Rachel's house, but had miraculously cleared up the minute Rachel stepped out of the front door.

"Can I give you a lift back to the Museum?" Rachel asked as she unlocked the car. "It's a bit out of my way, but Gerald's working overtime tonight, so it doesn't matter so much if I get home later than I'd like."

Even when she was offering to do Thelma a favour,

Rachel managed to word it like she was being put out and Thelma was being a massive inconvenience. She'd learned that from her mother. It never ceased to amaze Thelma how mothers shaped their children, moulding them in ways that turned them into mini versions of themselves. No wonder Thelma had turned out the way she had. Her own mother had been a complete nightmare.

"If it's not too much bother," Thelma said stiffly. "It looks like it's going to rain, and the Museum's a good hour-and-a-half walk from here."

"But it would only be about fifteen minutes on the bus," Rachel countered, pausing with her hand on the door as if giving Thelma the chance to reconsider her offer.

Thelma bit her lip. She hated it when Rachel did this. Rachel knew very well that Thelma was on such a tight budget that getting the bus would be an extra expense she couldn't afford. It was as though she deliberately put Thelma in situations where she had to admit as much, only to prove how generous Rachel was when she pulled out her own purse and gave her the bus fare or whatever charity it was that Thelma seemed in need of.

Thelma refused to play the game this time. She'd already done her bit coming to the cemetery. The least Rachel could do was give Thelma a lift in her expensive car to one of the many jobs she had to do to make ends meet.

"A lift would be great, Rachel. Thanks for offering," Thelma said, giving her a tight smile as she opened the door and sat down in the passenger seat. Rachel didn't say anything more, but her small frown as she clipped in her seatbelt told Thelma that Rachel thought she was being selfish.

They drove back through the city in silence. Beyond the small talk they managed to make while Thelma cleaned the house or prepared food, the two women had little in common. They hadn't been friends in school, and their lives were so dissimilar, they moved in completely different circles. Not that Thelma had a circle of her own. She had no partner, no friends, and her mother had died a decade ago leaving nothing to her daughter but bin bags full of clothes and charity-shop tat for Thelma to offload at the local dump.

If only I had a baby, Thelma thought longingly, watching parents walking their children home from the park for dinner, or sitting with them in the windows of the fast-food restaurants they drove past. *Someone to love and look after. Someone who would love me back. Someone who would think I was special. I wonder what a baby of my very own would look like? That would depend on the father, I suppose.*

She tried to imagine how a baby produced with any

of the men of her casual acquaintance would turn out. Dave, the previous night guard, would've probably given her an overweight little brat who sat glued to the TV all day. Andy, the other night guard, had kids of his own, and from what she'd seen of their pictures in the staffroom, they'd all inherited his weak chin. Old Harry who manned the front desk already had three grandchildren, and they were probably all as pasty-faced and boring as he was.

It was only men like Rachel's husband, Gerald, who seemed to produce the golden children that Thelma longed for. Men who were clever and confident and moved through the world with ease, as though they knew their place was at the very top of the social hierarchy. Thelma longed to have a child with someone like that. A golden child of her very own.

Knowing my luck, my baby would inherit my looks instead of his father's, Thelma thought morosely, pulling down the sun visor to check her reflection in the mirror. It wasn't just her own unattractive face she saw staring back at her. There was something sitting on the back seat. Something formless and lumpen, with strange hollows where its eyes and head should have been.

"What the..?"

Thelma lurched so suddenly around in her seat to look back it made Rachel swerve across the road into the oncoming rush-hour traffic.

"What the hell are you doing?" Rachel shrieked over the honking of horns and screeching of brakes.

"There's something behind us! It's…" Thelma peered into the gloom, uncertain now. It was late November, and even though it wasn't yet five o'clock, it was pitch black outside. The back seat was in shadow, lit only by the headlamps of passing cars.

Rachel steered the car to the side of the road, pulling up to the kerb and flicking the interior light on with shaking hands. "What did you think you were doing, Thelma?" she demanded. It wasn't just her hands that were shaking. There was a tremor of barely concealed fury in her voice. "You could've got us both killed!"

"I thought I saw something on the back seat!" Thelma protested. Now that she could see clearly in the double glow of the interior light and the streetlamp they were parked under, she saw that she'd been wrong. There was nothing on the back seat. She'd just mistaken the flash of headlamps on the shiny leather upholstery for something more.

Rachel took a deep breath, her knuckles white on the steering wheel. Thelma thought she was just trying to calm her nerves after the close brush with the oncoming cars, but when she spoke again, she realised Rachel had been psyching herself up for something far worse than a lecture about Thelma overreacting.

"Look, Thelma, I didn't want to bring this up now,

not with Christmas coming and everything, but the thing is," Rachel began, staring out of the windscreen instead of at Thelma, "we really don't need you working for us anymore."

"But…" Thelma opened and closed her mouth, unable to find the words to express her dismay.

"Gerald's mother was going to come over from the States to help out for a few months when the baby was born. Now that's not happening," Rachel frowned, soldiering bravely on, "but we've talked it over, and his mother would still like to move in with us. We both think it's a great idea. With Gerald's father passing a few years ago, she's been feeling lonely, and wants to move back here to the UK. We'll be trying for another baby soon, but in the meantime, I'm going back to my teaching job next week. She'll be helping around the house when I'm out, and she'll be company for me when Gerald's working late shifts."

"Aren't I company for you?"

Thelma wanted Rachel to hear how upset she was, to make her feel sympathy, or even pity. But as usual, her voice betrayed her, her words coming out as a petulant whine that set Rachel's teeth on edge.

"Of course, but we're both so… And Gerald's mother is…"

Rachel didn't need to finish. Thelma knew exactly what she meant. Thelma was a high-school dropout renting a council house who cleaned other people's toilets for a living, while Gerald's mother had been a distinguished surgeon before she retired. Rachel didn't want Thelma's company. She just wasn't on her level. She'd only taken Thelma on as yet another act of sanctimonious charity.

"I'll send you a full month's pay as a severance package, of course," Rachel said quickly, "and a little bonus for helping me out today. It was kind of you to come with me to Jonathan's grave."

Thelma clenched her firsts, quietly seething in the passenger seat at Rachel's words. *So that was why you wanted me to come*, she thought to herself. *So you could fire me straight after when I'd look like a horrible person if I said anything while you were still crying over your dead baby. You self-centred bitch!*

Thelma realised Rachel was still talking. When she glanced over, she saw Rachel's frown had been replaced by the bright look of breezy efficiency that was one step away from the cheerful smile she'd always worn. She clearly thought the danger of an unpleasant scene had passed, and had already moved on.

"...and if you could give the spare key back to me, that'd be really helpful – so I don't need to get another one cut for Gerald's mother arriving on Sunday."

"Sunday..?"

You've been planning this for ages, haven't you?

Thelma realised. *All those times you lay in bed pretending I was indispensable, and you were plotting the whole time to replace me with your oh-so-perfect mother-in-law.*

"I don't have the key on me," Thelma said stiffly, swallowing all the nasty words that were bubbling up from the back of her throat. "I didn't bring it as I knew you'd be in today."

"Oh, well, if you could post it to me, that would be great," Rachel said, already turning the engine on again and easing the car back into the flow of traffic.

"Post it?" Thelma felt a barely contained wave of fury surge through her at Rachel's dismissive words.

"Yes, it'll save you an extra trip to my house just to leave it off. There's no point coming all the way over just for that, is there?"

"No, I suppose there isn't," Thelma echoed dutifully, her flat words hiding the white-hot rage building to bursting point inside her chest.

"Ah, here we are. You don't mind walking across the park, do you?" Rachel said, pulling up by the university. "The traffic on the other side of the bridge is such a nightmare at this time of the evening. Anyway, I've really appreciated all your help this past year, and I wish you best of luck."

With that, Thelma was dismissed. Holding her tongue to avoid ruining her chances of the bonus month's pay as well as to spare her own dignity, Thelma merely gave Rachel a curt farewell and slammed the passenger door.

As she watched the taillights of Rachel's expensive car melting back into the river of traffic, she felt the first spots of heavy rain fall on her face. She didn't have an umbrella. She couldn't afford a fancy one, and the cheap ones from the pound shop kept breaking in the wind. She pulled up the hood of her thin jacket and trudged across the grass on the long, dark walk across the park that would spare Rachel a whole five extra minutes in traffic.

5.

Thelma wasn't alone on tonight's cleaning shift at the Museum.

The other cleaners were still on strike, the security guards and curators were down in their offices as usual, and the galleries had been shrouded in silence since the last of the visitors had left at closing time. But Thelma knew hers wasn't the only presence on the upper floors.

She'd noticed it as she polished the cases housing the Egyptian displays. At first it was just a hint of a shadow on the glass that made her turn, a strange formless flicker in the corner that was there one moment and gone the next.

There was nothing to be seen when she turned the main lights on briefly to take a good look, but she could've sworn she sensed something slithering along behind her as she wheeled her cart across the central hall.

The sightings became more frequent as she worked her way through the labyrinth of rooms – a reflection on a display case, a hint of movement mirrored in the polished frame of a painting, the shifting of a shadow behind a plinth as she rolled her cart past.

Thelma wasn't an easily frightened women – her hard life left her little mental space to indulge in superstitious fancies. But by the time she reached the taxidermy room, her hands were shaking as they gripped the handle of her cart and every nerve in her body was stretched to breaking point.

It wasn't fear of the unknown that filled her with dread as she crossed the room to the cabinet housing the black bear. It was the utter certainty of knowing exactly what it was that haunted her footsteps, shadowing her every move. She'd first suspected it that night she'd seen a shape moving in the black bear's display case. The trip to the cemetery with Rachel had confirmed her suspicions. And after what she'd glimpsed on the back seat of the car…

"What is it?" Thelma demanded, rapping on the glass

case, trying to sound defiant despite her trembling hands. "What do you want with me?"

Even before the bear moved its head, staring back at her with dead fire in its eyes, Thelma already knew the answer. A low growl filled the room – or perhaps Thelma only imagined that the sound in her ears was coming from outside? The words were as formless as the lumpen shape that lurked in the shadows behind her, but Thelma seemed to recognise their meaning. They spoke of a deep longing that mirrored her own – dark and selfish and willing to do whatever it took to get what it wanted.

Thelma's shoulders relaxed as the growl deepened, filling her with the confidence and certainty she'd been longing for her whole life. All the petty worries of her miserable daily toil fell away, and she felt lighter than she'd ever done before. She knew now what her purpose was. She was no longer that charity-shop child, the cast off no one wanted around. She no longer felt inferior to the people who'd looked down on her for her whole life.

She was special. She was *chosen.*

She'd show Rachel and Holly and all the stuck-up bitches like them that *she* – Thelma Smithson – was a better woman than any of them. She'd show all the men who had ever rejected her just how fruitful her slowly withering womb could be.

Starting with Rachel's husband, Gerald.

"Yes," she whispered back to the voice that growled from the hollow void where the bear's cub had once been growing. "Yes, I understand what must be done."

The growl grew soft, a rumbling caress that made Thelma shiver with longing for what was to come.

When she gazed back at the glass case, the bear was frozen once more, no longer moving, and the formless shadow that had flickered in the corner of her eye was gone. But what she saw reflected back at her was even better.

There was a smile on her lined face – a smile more powerful and more triumphant than the simpering little smirk that Rachel Benson had been charming people with since she was a child.

Thelma licked her lips, eagerly anticipating the shape of things to come.

6.

Rachel wasn't at home the next day when Thelma put her spare key in the lock and opened Rachel's front door. She'd known Rachel would be out – she'd leafed through her diary the last time she'd been in to clean and had seen that Rachel had a lunchtime date with some school friends today. That was the kind of thing people like Rachel did – stayed in touch with all the fawning little drones who'd buzzed around their queen bee back in those distant school days, rewarding them for their loyalty with her attention over coffee now and then.

Thelma had never been invited on any of those lunch dates. No one 'friended' her on social media, let alone in real life. As far as the popular girls from school were concerned, she'd been just another nameless bit player in the drama of their lives.

Not for much longer, Thelma thought. *Soon they'll all know just how important I am.*

She climbed the stairs, glancing at the many photo frames arranged in a tasteful diagonal all the way up to the landing. Pictures of Rachel and Gerald graduating. Pictures of exotic holidays on camels, on tropical beaches and at famous landmarks. Cosy pictures of family parties with in-laws and oh-so-many celebrations with numerous friends whose perfect hair and white teeth gleamed back at Thelma in a scornful rebuke of her own plain face and humdrum life.

This time, Thelma didn't feel rage or resentment. Instead, there was only the gloating anticipation of what was to come. She'd been so wrong to think they were better than her, to let them treat her as though they were better. Soon she'd have what she dreamed of, and their superficial little lives and petty achievements wouldn't mean anything at all.

She continued on down the landing. The house was large and the hallway led in a wide sweep of spotless carpeting from the palatial master bedroom to the spare room, each with their own ensuite bathrooms. It was the room at the end of the hall that Thelma was heading for. The room she hadn't been allowed into since Rachel lost her baby.

Thelma had respected her wishes until now. Not that she'd had much choice – Rachel had always been in the house while she'd been cleaning over the past few weeks. But Rachel wasn't here now, and Thelma didn't have to do as she was told anymore.

She could do whatever she wanted. She could *have* whatever she wanted.

A frisson of anticipation ran up her spine as she turned the handle and pushed the door open.

The nursery was painted blue in expectation of the boy Rachel had been carrying. There was a playpen full of toys in one corner, and a wardrobe and matching chest of drawers against the opposite wall, both full of baby clothes. But it was the cradle in the centre of the room that Thelma had come here to see.

The curtains were closed, the room shrouded in respectful shade to mark the passing of the golden dream Rachel and her husband once had. Thelma's dream didn't need light. It was a dream of formless shadows hidden in the dark.

As she stepped into the room, the cradle began to rock gently to and fro, as though stirred by an invisible breeze. Thelma approached slowly, reverently, her excitement reaching fever pitch when she leaned down and saw the shapeless mass that lay quivering beneath the blue blankets. It wasn't ready – not yet. It needed Thelma to breathe new life into its premature carcass.

Thelma and…someone else.

Thelma heard the front door close on the floor below, a soft thump as items were laid on the dining room table, then the thud of footsteps on the stairs. She knew whose feet that confident tread belonged to. She'd seen the note clearly in Rachel's diary. The last hour of her lunch date with her friends would coincide with Gerald's half-day off. The diary said he'd go to the gym for the hour. But Thelma would make sure he had a different kind of workout than the one he'd planned.

"What the..? Oh, it's you, Thelma." Gerald stood in the doorway, a frown on his handsome face as he stared at the woman half shrouded in darkness. "I thought you'd already finished working here?"

Before, Thelma would have shrunk under his self-assured stare. She would have mumbled an apology, her shoulders stooping to make herself as small and unobtrusive as possible. But not today. Today she looked him right in the eye, her own gaze steady and the powerful smile she'd been gifted the night before playing on her lips.

For the first time, Gerald looked uncertain as he stared back at her. "Well then," he blustered, "I take it you've come to return the key?"

When Thelma didn't respond, he became even more nervous, as though she was sucking the confidence from him, draining him of all the force of will she'd once envied.

"Look, you really shouldn't be in here. Rachel wouldn't like it, and…"

He stopped, his face going slack. Thelma was growling at him. It was a low sound that rumbled up his spine, shaking him to the very core. His eyes took on a glassy look, somehow reminiscent of a dead animal hollowed out and filled with foreign matter where its living essence had once been. A fog of musk seemed to fill the room, the soft notes of perfume heightened by the sharp tang of a she-bear in heat.

As though compelled by forces beyond his control, Gerald moved forward, his arms outstretched to receive the woman who rushed to meet his embrace.

And as the two writhed in a shapeless mass on the bedroom floor, another formless shadow began to move, wriggling and slithering its way out of the cradle towards them.

7.

Five months later, Holly, the young intern, had a full-time job as assistant curator. Her status was higher, and her salary was increased accordingly. But she was no longer bossing Thelma around. In fact, none of the curators or museum staff seemed incline to talk down to the cleaner anymore.

"Oh, you're busy in here? Well, I'll come back later, then."

Holly stopped dead at the entrance to the taxidermy room, a flicker of what looked like alarm crossing her face as she saw Thelma quietly working away with her mop and bucket.

Thelma didn't reply. She just smiled at Holly – a powerful, knowing smile that seemed to both command respect and repel the young assistant curator at the same time. Thelma knew that Holly needed access to the cabinets to change some of the displays in the room. But Holly's work could wait. She wasn't the important one anymore. Thelma was the one with all the authority now.

"Um, should you be doing all that lifting, you know, in your condition?" Holly asked nervously, trying to avert her eyes from the bulge in Thelma's navy uniform. Thelma said nothing. She just smiled back at her until Holly muttered something awkward about having paperwork to file and dashed for the stairs.

It wasn't just Holly who found Thelma's presence unnerving. The other cleaners had been avoiding her ever since their strike ended in a stalemate rather than the pay rise they'd been holding out for. Thelma glanced up as one of the women passed along the gallery outside with her own cart. The older cleaner had always hen-pecked Thelma before. Now she looked cowed, keeping her head down and her eyes on the floor as she hurried to a different section of the museum. No one liked to look Thelma in the eye anymore. And no one liked to talk openly about fact that Thelma had outgrown her uniform so completely that it gaped open all down its front fastenings. There was something almost obscene about the swelling of Thelma's belly, something that made people look away and mutter to each other rather than ask her all the usual congratulatory questions about how she was feeling and when she was due.

If they had asked, Thelma would have told them she felt stronger and more in control than she'd ever believed possible. And as for when she was due…well, the new life would come when it was ready, and not a moment before.

It had been a happy day. She'd gone for her first ultrasound. She should have had one months ago, but she hadn't wanted to share her secret with the world, not until she was showing. The nurse had turned pale when she'd stared at the monitor and then run straight for the doctor, and the doctor had looked queasy when he saw for himself what was growing inside Thelma. He'd sat down heavily and run through all her options for termination, and Thelma had smiled beatifically the whole time, her eyes fixed firmly on the shapeless, quivering mass that filled the screen.

Her baby wouldn't be golden like Rachel's would have been, but it was all hers. Hers to form. Hers to mould into exactly the shape she wanted.

She wasn't sure if Gerald remembered his part in its creation, but it didn't matter. He'd served his purpose. Thelma didn't even care about getting revenge on Rachel by telling her she was pregnant. It wasn't really her husband's child, not in the way that actually mattered. All of those concerns about social hierarchy seemed so petty and pointless now. And besides, she'd heard that Rachel and Gerald had moved to the States last month. There were whisperings that their golden marriage was crumbling, but that didn't concern Thelma now either.

All that mattered, was that she had what she wanted herself.

As she polished the glass of the largest taxidermy case containing her favourite specimen, she laid a hand on her swollen belly, humming a soft song that echoed through the silent, after-hours corridors of the Museum like the distant, rumbling growl of a bear.

THE SHAPE OF THE BEAST

THE WHISPERING SHELL

1.

"...And that, boys and girls, is the water cycle. Does anyone have any questions they'd like to ask before we finish?"

The boy who'd pushed two smaller children out of the way so he could claim the beanbag at the front of the group stuck up his hand. "If all water's connected, does that mean every time Stuart has a drink of water, he's drinking my pee?"

Julie smiled wearily as the restless group of school children erupted in a chorus of sniggers. There was always one. "In a way," she said through a tight-lipped grin. "Not directly of course, but with everything being connected, you could say that every time you drink a can of coke that's been made with water from the cycle, you're drinking his pee as well."

The laughter now descended into groans of disgust. Julie sensed she'd lost the room, and looked to the group's teacher to sort the noise out. He glanced up from the phone he'd been scrolling through while she gave her talk, a 'thanks for nothing' scowl on his face.

"Alright, settle down," he said wearily. "If you

don't behave, we'll go straight back to the bus instead of visiting the gift shop first."

Knowing an empty threat when they heard one, the group of ten year olds continued to jeer at each other, pushing and shoving as the insults of 'pee drinker' and 'you just washed your hands in my pee!' got louder.

Julie heaved a sigh, thanking her lucky stars that she'd failed the interview for the teacher training course twenty-five years ago. She'd been a painfully shy teenager, and had stuttered and stammered so much through the assessment day she'd barely got a sentence out. Given how desperate the education department was for new recruits, even that might not have been enough to get her rejected, had she not got so nervous during the final group assignment that she'd burst into tears in front of the whole interview panel.

She still remembered clearly her mother's disgusted face when the rejection letter had arrived.

"So that's another thing you've failed at, then?" she'd spat out, shaking her head in despair. *"How am I supposed to face my friends now? What am I going to tell them? My daughter's going to spend the rest of her life at the supermarket checkout tills? No, you couldn't even do that, could you, because that would require you to speak to other people."*

A quarter of a century had passed, and Julie's stomach still knotted in anger and shame at the memory.

It hadn't been fair. She'd been a good student, and had got decent exam grades. But she was too shy to join the drama group, failed the audition for the school choir, and had a massive panic attack during the try-outs for the debating team that had resulted in a trip to the nurse's room and a phone call to her mother's office. Her mother had refused to leave work to pick her up, telling the nurse to stop mollycoddling her daughter or she'd never amount to anything. Her voice had been so loud and strident Julie had heard the other half of the phone conversation clearly. Even if she hadn't, she'd known what her mother would say, and could picture the disappointment on her face clearly.

Her mother had wanted a daughter who would follow in her footsteps. That didn't necessarily mean becoming a top-flight lawyer like her, but she did expect Julie to be gregarious and popular, with a large group of friends and a busy social life. She'd never bothered to hide her dissatisfaction at the nervous, self-conscious introvert she'd got instead. And she'd never seen Julie's degree in Heritage Studies as anything other than another lame excuse to avoid getting a proper job and living in the real world.

This IS a proper job, Julie told herself, repeating the self-affirming mantra her therapist advised her to fall back on every time she heard her mother's critical voice in her head. *I'm a well-respected member of the*

Museum team, and I've even worked my way up to giving talks to school groups. I AM a success, and I HAVE become a confident and strong person.

All the positive affirmations in the world couldn't stop her feeling sick with nerves at the sight of the unruly children gathered in the natural history section, though. The little brat at the front of the group was now lifting his beanbag over his head, intending to clobber the smaller boy called Stuart with it.

"ENOUGH!" their teacher bellowed. "Ryan, put that down NOW! Line up at the door, everyone. We'll have ten minutes in the gift shop, then it's time to leave."

And that, right there, is why your class doesn't listen to you, Julie grumbled to herself as the children pushed and shoved their way out of the room in a vague semblance of a line. *You can't expect them to take you seriously if you don't follow through on punishment threats.*

Julie knew that was true, because she'd read every parenting manual she could get her hands on before her son, Oliver, was born. She didn't want to repeat her own mother's mistakes. Even with doing everything differently, he'd still grown up a mini version of Julie, complete with all of her shyness, social diffidence and neurotic tendencies.

At least he's not like my mother was, Julie thought. *That would've been worse.*

Julie sucked in a deep breath, trying to tame the snakes of anxiety that writhed in her stomach as silence settled back on the natural history room once more. She didn't know why she got so worked up about talking to school groups – they were just *kids*, for God's sake! But every time she was scheduled to give a half-hour talk as part of the Museum's educational outreach program, she tossed and turned in her bed all night, unable to sleep with nerves.

At least that's another talk over – no more until next week, she thought, piling the beanbags up in the corner and frowning when she saw that Ryan had managed to tear a hole in the one he'd been sitting on.

She was just going to check that the wayward students hadn't damaged any of the shells or fossils she'd laid out on the sensory table, when she realised she wasn't alone. There was a small girl standing at the table, holding one of the shells to her ear and listening with such an intense look of concentration on her face that Julie almost laughed. She'd let each of the children have their turn of 'listening to the sound of the waves' in the shell, but most had passed it on with a bored scowl and a rude comment when they realised it wasn't the interactive surround-sound experience they'd come to expect from their video games, and they'd have to actually use their own imaginations to conjure a vision of the sea.

At least there are some still kids who aren't completely jaded, she thought with a smile. *What's the point of childhood if there isn't any magic in it?*

The little girl reminded Julie of herself at that age – with the same serious look in her eyes and the same need to keep her distance from the other children. She almost felt guilty interrupting her quiet moment of reflection and making her rejoin the group of unruly students she was clearly desperate to keep away from.

"Your teacher's already gone downstairs, pet," Julie said gently. "It's time for you to go down to the gift shop."

The girl didn't respond. In fact, it was almost as though she hadn't heard Julie speak at all. Julie knelt down so she was eye to eye with the girl.

"Did you hear me, pet? The talk's over, you need to go downstairs and join your class." She reached out for the shell, taking hold of it gently. The girl shuddered, as though waking up and seeing Julie for the first time.

"What were you listening to?" Julie asked, seeing the girl blinking as she glanced around the room, a puzzled frown on her face. "Could you hear the sea?"

"No, it was the taps running," the girl said softly. "She said she was cold. She said I should get in the bath so we could be together."

Julie stared at the little girl, her smile turning to an uneasy frown. "Bath taps..?" she said slowly. "No, pet, the whooshing sound is just the noise that trapped air makes because of the shape of the shell. It's supposed to sound like waves on a beach."

The girl shook her head slowly, her eyes still wide. "But she wasn't on the beach when it happened. She was in the bath. The taps were running."

Julie opened her mouth to ask what she meant, when the girl's harassed-looking teacher hurried back into the room. "Ruby? There you are! I've been looking everywhere. Hurry up, it's time to get on the bus."

The girl finally let go of the shell reluctantly and followed her teacher out, glancing back over her shoulder with an uneasy look on her face as Julie rearranged the objects on the sensory table.

That's some imagination she's got, Julie thought to herself. *She's going to grow up to be a writer or an artist, I'll bet. I just hope her family don't shame her for daydreaming and being a bit different from the other kids.*

Julie would have liked to have been a writer or an artist. She'd learned very early on, though, that her mother didn't approve of imaginations. Those were for people who studied useless, arty subjects at university and spent their whole lives scraping by on low-paid jobs, according to her. Subjects like Heritage Studies. Jobs like the one Julie had been working in ever since she graduated. She'd thought her mother would have been proud when she announced she'd got a job at the Museum following a successful internship. She only learned years later that her mother had been telling all her friends that Julie worked as an accountant for a well-known financial company.

It wasn't the sting of her mother's lies or the fact she'd made no secret of how ashamed she was of Julie's low salary that made Julie's frown deepen now, though. It was the sight of two damaged shells and one fossil broken into pieces that made her snort angrily.

Little brats! she thought. Kids were off the rails these days. Thank God she hadn't gone into teaching after all. And thank God Oliver was a good-natured, eager-to-please boy, not like the unruly, entitled little monsters she found herself dealing with in the school outreach groups.

At least it's just a plaster model, she sighed to herself, brushing the crumbled remains of the fossil into the bin and making a note to replace it. But the shells were real, and she examined the conch carefully to make sure its impressive spiral and frilled edges were intact. It was her favourite shell in the collection, and she wished she could keep it out of the careless hands of schoolchildren, but the Director liked to encourage a more interactive approach to the displays than the Museum had when Julie had first started her job here.

I wonder what she meant, she thought, her mind

turning back to the little girl who'd remained to listen to the wind whispering in the shell. *Running taps in the bath? It doesn't sound anything like that.*

She raised the shell to her ear, listening carefully. The trapped air murmured softly, reminding her of childhood trips to the beach. She hadn't liked the water back then. It had been cold and she was self-conscious about her body, hating having to strip off and walk around in a tight swimsuit. It had been yet another opportunity for her mother to prod her stomach and tell her she was spending too much time in her room eating biscuits instead of exercising in the fresh air. Her disgust at Julie's hesitation on the water's edge had always been palpable, a twice-yearly ritual of humiliation that had become such a well-established pantomime, Julie could still recite the lines off by heart.

She wasn't sure now why she'd agreed to join her mother for a holiday with Oliver at the same spot last summer. Maybe she thought she owed it to her, after keeping her at arm's length since he was born. Or maybe she'd let her mother's accusations that she was denying her son the chance of a relationship with his only surviving grandparent to guilt trip her into it. Either way, she'd regretted it, and not just for the tragic way the holiday had ended.

The waves sounded just the same as they did that day she went swimming before breakfast, Julie realised with a start. *They were breaking against the shore with more force than usual. The tide was strong. She shouldn't have gone out. She should have listened when I told her...*

Julie put the conch shell down quickly, the sound of distant waves unsettling her. The past couldn't be undone. She might not have the chance now to prove to her mother that she wasn't a disappointment, but at least the therapy was helping her work though some of the damage her mother had done to her over the years.

Glancing at her watch, she realised she'd already missed ten minutes of her lunch break. With a last fuss over the sensory table to line up the shells and fossils just the way she liked them, she hurried down the stairs to the staffroom and the sandwich that was waiting for her in the fridge.

2.

It was in the staffroom, a week later, that Julie heard the terrible news.

Betty, one of the security guards on the day shift, was passing round the local newspaper and telling the story afresh each time someone new came in for lunch. Julie just caught the tail-end of one recital, but what she heard was enough to send chills down her spine.

"What's the world coming to, when a ten year old

goes and does that?" Betty was saying, half upset, half indignant. "How did she get hold of the pills, that's what I want to know. Her poor father. He was only just getting over his wife's death."

"What happened?" Julie asked. The reproachful glances the three young interns threw her told her they'd already heard the story several times now and would prefer to finish their lunch in peace rather than listen to it again.

"Here, it's in the paper." One of them handed Julie the well-thumbed local newspaper, already open at the appropriate page. One glance was enough to shake Julie to the core. It wasn't just the headline, 'School Pupil Dies in Tragic Repeat of Mother's Suicide' that made her shudder. It was the eyes that stared back at her from the page. She knew the girl in the photograph was called Ruby. She remembered that's what her teacher had called her the other week when he came to collect her from the natural history room.

"Seems her mum committed suicide a few years back – slit her wrists in the bath. The little girl was the one who found her. Been carrying that weight around with her ever since. Can you imagine what that does to a child?" Betty took the paper from Julie before she'd had a chance to read it, giving Julie her own version of the story. "Social services should've helped that family out. There's no support for kids with mental health issues these days."

Julie knew that only too well. She had to pay privately for Oliver's counselling sessions to manage his anxiety, as well as her own therapy. Her doctor had said the NHS waiting list was eighteen months, and that was if she managed to find a place for him at all.

"And the little girl, did she commit suicide too, the same as her mother?" The thought was so horrible that Julie could hardly get the words out.

Betty nodded grimly. "Well, almost the same. She didn't slit her wrists. It was pills she took in the bath – somehow got them out of her father's locked medicine cabinet. Oh, don't bother, none of that's in the newspaper," she said, throwing it down on the table before Julie could read the story for herself.

"Then how do you—"

"Got a granddaughter at the same school, haven't I? Not in the same class, luckily," Betty said with obvious relief. "Three years below, but it's the only thing being talked about at the school gates, and no wonder. My poor little Lucy's been in tears about it for days. It's a scandal that they haven't offered proper counselling to all the children, just the ones in the girl's class. Don't know what we bother paying our taxes for if the Council can't even cover the cost of looking after our little ones when something terrible happens and they need to talk to a professional. Aw, love, are you alright?"

She finally came to a halt, noticing that Julie's face had gone chalk white as she stared at the picture looking back at her from the open newspaper.

"Yes, it's just… I saw that little girl. She was in the school group that was here for a talk last week. She was holding one of our shells, and…" Julie put a hand over her mouth, feeling a sudden urge to be sick.

"Sit down there, love, I'll get you a cup of tea," Betty said, mercifully closing the newspaper on her way to the sink.

Julie stared at the floor, feeling the eyes of the younger interns on her. They were all embarrassed, not knowing what to say. None of them had children yet. None of them knew the awful, crushing fear that came with hearing of another child's death. It was a terrible reminder that her own child was mortal and death could come and claim him at any moment.

"Here you go." Betty handed her a steaming mug of tea, hovering in a motherly way to make sure she drank it without spilling it on her skirt.

No, not in a motherly way. Just in a kind way, Julie thought sadly. *My mother would never have acted like that. She would've told me to pull myself together and stop embarrassing her.*

Another, darker thought flashed across her head before she could stop it.

Maybe it's just as well that my mother isn't here anymore.

"Will you be OK to take the group this afternoon?" Betty interrupted her thoughts before she could sink into a bog of guilt and remorse at her own treachery. "I'm sure the school wouldn't mind it being cancelled, if you call them early enough."

Julie shook her head, the warm tea reviving her. "It's fine, I'll be OK. It's always such a shock when you hear things like that, isn't it? Makes you think…"

She didn't need to finish. Betty understood completely. She had three children of her own and seven grandchildren. She wasn't embarrassed by Julie's overaction the way the young interns were.

"I'd best go and get set up," Julie said, getting up quickly to escape their unwanted scrutiny. "There's a big group coming, and I have to make sure there's enough seats or there'll be arguments. You know what kids are like."

Betty nodded again, while the interns just looked blank.

"Aren't you going to have your lunch first?" Betty asked as Julie headed for the door.

"I'm not hungry. It's just a sandwich. It'll keep for later."

And the sooner she got away from the newspaper with its tragic news and picture of that poor little girl, the better.

3.

The afternoon talk wasn't as bad as Julie feared. The class, although large, was reasonably well behaved, and Julie was confident enough they weren't going to deliberately break anything to let them loose to wander around the displays on their own for ten minutes after she'd finished her own presentation.

The teacher looked tired and harassed, but at least she was paying attention to the children in her charge instead of using Julie's presence as an excuse to play on her phone. Julie felt more relaxed with this class than she'd done in a long time, and had almost started to enjoy their eager questions, when she noticed something odd. There was a small boy standing by the sensory table, the conch shell clamped to his ear. He had the same look of intense concentration on his face that Ruby had the week before.

Without knowing why, a strange sense of foreboding gripped Julie. She left the group that was crowding around the dinosaur fossils in a glass case, and hurried over to the sensory table.

"Are you alright there?" she asked the boy. He looked up at her, his eyes wide. Then he shook his head slowly.

"Billy says I need to come and be with him. He says

he's lonely."

"And who's Billy?" Julie glanced back at the other children who were milling around the exhibits in the large room.

"He's my brother," the boy said, his ear still clamped to the shell.

"Oh. And is he at the same school?"

"No," the boy said, his eyes still locked on hers. "He's dead."

Before Julie could react, the teacher called for everyone's attention. "Right, we've only got fifteen minutes left. We're going to visit the gift shop in a group, but those of you who need to stop at the loo, please go with Miss Anderson here," she nodded at the classroom assistant who'd done a sterling job of keeping some of the more boisterous children in check. "It's a long drive back to school, so go now if you need to."

The other children started to line up at the door, but the small boy with the shell stood where he was, his head tilted to one side as he listened intently to the air whooshing inside. Julie waved to get the teacher's attention. This was something she felt should be dealt with by someone who knew the child.

"He's talking about his dead brother," she whispered to the teacher when she came over. "Was it recent?"

"No, it was a swimming pool accident when he was

too small to remember it," the teacher whispered back. "He's never mentioned it in class before, but his parents told the school about it when he started his first year, just in case it ever came up. Thanks for the heads up, I'll keep an eye on him. Jayden," she said aloud, "it's time to go downstairs. Would you like to come and look at the books in the shop with me?"

The boy hesitated, the conch shell still clutched tightly in his hand. Then his eyes flicked to the other end of the room where the classroom assistant was rounding children up for a bathroom break. "No," he said softly, as though finally making up his mind about something. "I'll go with Miss Anderson."

"Let's just put this back down first, shall we?" Julie said gently, easing his fingers from the shell and setting it on the table. It wasn't the first time that she'd had to rescue the natural history room's objects from the sticky mitts of small children or the pockets and bags of people old enough to know better, but at least this time it seemed to be a genuine mistake. The boy really did look a little confused, like he wasn't quite sure where he was.

Julie followed the group out, watching them head down the stairs then split into two groups, the larger one heading for the gift shop with the teacher while the smaller group headed towards the large 'toilets' sign.

Poor boy, she thought. *It must have been that story in*

the news that's brought everything back up again for the family. I'm sure his parents have been talking about it. He might not remember it, but his parents will still be grieving.

For the second time that day she felt the cold hand of death brush uncomfortably close to the stable life that she'd built for herself and her son. She hated being reminded of mortality. She'd thought her mother with her infinite well of disapproval would last forever, but the holiday last summer had proved without a shadow of a doubt that even the most permanent things in life were fleeting.

Rearranging the sensory table, Julie couldn't help picking up the conch shell again and examining it. It wasn't one of the smaller, more compact ones that were usually found around the beaches of the British Isles – the ones that Oliver said looked like mini unicorn horns. He liked to collect shells when they were on the beach. In fact, he'd found this very shell for his collection during their last holiday in the summer. He'd been tripping over himself with excitement to show her his precious find. It had clearly been washed up from more distant, tropical shores, and they'd gone back to the hotel room to look it up on the internet. That's when the police had knocked on the door and given them the news that—

Julie set the shell down with a thump. No wonder

Oliver hadn't wanted to keep it after that. In fact, he'd bagged up his entire collection and shoved it in the bin as soon as they'd got home. She'd rescued the best shells and put them in the shed just in case he changed his mind. But this one she'd kept for the museum. It was a real beauty – it deserved to be on display.

It was odd, though, the way both Ruby and Jayden had said strange things after putting it to their ear.

It must be the association with water, she thought, picking up the shell again and turning it over in her hands. She'd put her ear to countless shells before on childhood beach holidays, but she'd never come across one that mimicked the sound of waves so clearly. They came and went, a soft sighing that seemed to grow louder and more forceful the longer she listened. And then there was that other sound. The murmur in the background that seemed almost like a voice calling her name.

Julie... Julie... Julie...

Julie set the shell down quickly. She was clearly just overtired. Knowing she was giving a school talk today had meant another night of insomnia and way too much coffee this morning. An early night was what she needed, and a good book to take her mind off that unpleasant newspaper story.

She was just turning off her Powerpoint presentation and unhooking the overhead projector screen leads from her laptop, when she heard the scream from downstairs.

4.

"And how have you been feeling at work since then?" her therapist asked, leaning forward in her chair.

Julie fidgeted. She hated talking about her emotions. It always made her feel weak and vulnerable. Her mother had always said she was too soft and needed to toughen up. Maybe she was right. Maybe if she'd listened to her mother, she wouldn't be feeling so awful right now.

"It's been…hard," Julie admitted, pushing the unwanted thoughts of her mother from her mind and trusting her therapist instead. "The police shut the Museum for four days while they conducted their investigations, but they decided in the end it was just a tragic accident. The family still want answers, of course, but I think that will mostly involve the school and what the two adults in charge of the group were doing at the time. The inquest will probably drag on for months. I'll probably have to give evidence in court."

Seeing her shudder at the thought, her therapist laid a hand on her arm. "And that scares you?" she asked gently.

Of course it bloody well scares me! Julie wanted to yell at the top of her voice. *Of course the thought of standing up in court and speaking about a child's death in front of all those people makes me feel sick!*

She didn't say that, though. She knew that would make her sound selfish. After all, the parents needed answers. Otherwise, how could they possibly come to terms with the fact that their child had drowned in the museum toilets on a supervised school trip?

She stared at the floor, taking deep breaths the way her therapist had taught her when the anxiety began to build to uncomfortable levels. She tried not to remember the scream that sent her running down the stairs. She tried not to remember racing across the central hall to the toilets where white-faced children were stumbling out, tears streaming down their terrified faces. She tried not to remember the panicked cries of the classroom assistant as she pulled desperately at the body of the small boy stuck with his head so far down one of the U-bends she couldn't get him out again without Julie's help.

Most of all, she tried not to remember the dead eyes of the drowned child staring back up at them when they laid him on the floor.

She tried so hard to block it all out she felt almost dizzy with effort.

"Have you thought about taking time off?" the therapist

suggested. "Going away on holiday for a while with your son?"

Holiday...

The sound of waves whooshed in Julie's ears, reminding her of last summer on the beach. There had been wailing sirens and the flashing lights of police cars back then too. She shuddered, wishing her doctor would just prescribes her pills to block it all out. Given her history of anxiety, though, he wasn't willing to give her anything but useless advice leaflets about NHS counselling sessions she wouldn't be able to access without waiting on endless lists. The cost of these private sessions was something else she was trying not to think about.

"No, I can't afford to take time off work," Julie said. It wasn't that she couldn't get medical leave. Given how long she'd worked at the Museum, they'd probably allow her a few months of that. But the presence of the eager young interns in the staffroom was a constant reminder that no one at the Museum was irreplaceable, and there was an endless supply of new talent to fill an ever-decreasing number of jobs in the arts sector. "Besides, it wouldn't be fair on Oliver, he needs the stability of school, especially after what happened last summer..."

Julie trailed off, wishing everything didn't always come back to her mother.

Her therapist noted her hesitation, and seized on it immediately.

"Did what happened last week bring back a lot of memories of your mother?" she asked. "Did you make upsetting connections between the two deaths?"

Three deaths, Julie silently corrected her. She hadn't mentioned the little girl who'd swallowed pills in the bath a few weeks ago. It had been emotionally draining enough just talking about Jayden's accident in the Museum toilets.

How could it have happened? she asked herself for the hundredth time. *How could he possibly have got his head stuck in the U-bend? The classroom assistant insisted he wasn't being bullied by the other boys, and there wasn't time for them to—*

"Julie?" the therapist prompted. "Did you hear what I asked?"

"Yes, I was thinking… Maybe it's just all this connection with water that seems strange."

Julie blinked at the same time the therapist did, not quite sure what her own words meant either.

"I'm sorry? Connection to water? You mean the accident at the beach, and the one in the Museum toilets?"

"Um, yes, and the water cycle – how water is all connected, and…" Julie trailed off, losing the threads of her own thoughts. The rain beat down against the windowpane, a bitter lament that had gone on for a week, almost as though the sky was in mourning for the boy who'd lost his life in such a senseless way.

"The water cycle..?"

The therapist was giving her that raised eyebrow look that told Julie the session was running over time but she didn't want to seem insensitive by pointing it out.

"Just something I teach in the educational outreach sessions," Julie muttered, gathering up her coat and handbag. "Thanks for today, it really helped," she lied.

"Just remember to continue with your CBT exercises over the next week, and if you need anything, call me," the therapist said, walking her to the door. Julie would have appreciated the offer a little more if it didn't mean paying the extra fees.

Oliver was already waiting for her in the reception area, his head resting on his hands as he stared at the abstract painting hanging on the wall opposite. He looked older than his nine years, as though the gravity of his thoughts had prematurely furrowed his brow and pulled his lips down at the corners. She'd rarely seen him smile, except when he'd been gathering shells on the beach. After last summer, even the thought of that once-cherished hobby was yet another source of distress for him.

"How did it go?" she asked, sitting down on the comfy

sofa next to him and pulling her son into a tight hug. "Did you have a chat about your father?"

Julie wished for his sake she'd been able to make her marriage work. But her husband had walked out on her when Oliver was two, preferring the company of a younger woman without a toddler who cried through the night. He'd moved to Australia and cut them both out of his life completely, like they were some kind of cancerous tumour he couldn't wait to be free from. He didn't even send Oliver a card on his birthdays. No wonder the poor boy needed therapy.

I guess that's what happens when you marry the first man who pays you any attention, Julie sighed to herself. She'd been so flattered by Tom's vague interest when they met at an art conservation workshop ten years ago that she'd practically thrown herself at him. Her therapist had helped her to see how that was her mother's doing too. Her mother might have looked down on Tom and warned her that he wasn't good husband material, but if she hadn't been so damn cold for all of Julie's life then maybe—

"We didn't talk about Dad, we talked about Granny," Oliver said softly.

"Oh." Julie waited. Oliver rarely talked to her about what happened last summer. Maybe he was finally ready to open up about how that disastrous holiday had affected him.

"He was asking why I thought I've been dreaming about Granny so often this week," Oliver said, his frown growing deeper as he struggled to process ideas that were too big for such a small boy.

Julie bit her lip. This was news to her. Oliver hadn't mentioned anything about his granny recently. Or maybe she'd been so busy trying to put on a brave face and hide the story about the drowned boy from her son that she hadn't noticed he'd been even quieter than usual. "And why do you think that is?" she prompted, hoping she hadn't accidentally let Oliver overhear one of her phone conversations with the Museum or her consultations with the police about the drowning. The last thing she wanted was to dredge up memories of the summer holiday at the beach.

"I said it was because of all the rain," Oliver shrugged, glancing at the window where water was streaming in endless little rivers.

"Oh." Julie said again. She waited another minute, but as nothing more was forthcoming, she said, "But it wasn't raining last summer. It was sunny the whole time we were at the beach."

"Yes, but water's all connected, isn't it?" Oliver said, turning to look at her for the first time. "That's what you're always saying."

Julie felt a sharp stab of guilt pierce her soul. Her son was upset and it was all her fault. She was the one who'd planted unwanted thoughts in his head without meaning to. It was her job to protect him from adult cares and worries, and she'd messed that up too. Her mother had been right. She was a complete failure.

I AM a success, and I HAVE become a confident and strong person, Julie tried chanting to herself. It was no good. Her therapist's positive affirmations rang hollow in her ears. She hadn't just failed at being a daughter. She'd failed at being a wife, and now she was failing at being a mother too.

I'm NOT a bad mother! she shouted at the nasty voice in her head that sounded suspiciously like her own mother's. *I know how to take care of my son.*

Routine was what they needed. A nice, safe, stable routine would help them both manage their anxiety and keep intrusive thoughts at bay. She took Oliver's hand and walked him back to the car, shielding him from the driving rain as best she could.

5.

They didn't get routine or stability. The following week the teachers across the city went on strike, demanding better working conditions and pay, and the schools were all closed. The Museum was accommodating, allowing Julie to bring Oliver into work with her as long as she supervised him at all times, but still, it wasn't exactly the return to normality she'd been hoping for.

The first few days were fine, with Julie bringing in books and colouring sheets to keep Oliver amused while she sat at her desk or updated her records. But by Wednesday, Oliver was getting restless, wanting to explore the many rooms and collections on his own and turning petulant when she told him he couldn't leave her side. The louring skies and never-ending rain added to the feeling of claustrophobia, and an oppressive atmosphere settled over the Museum, deepening the gloom the staff had all been feeling since the young schoolboy's tragic accident. Visitors were few and far between, put off travelling by the flood warnings that had been issued in many areas and the constant disruptions to public transport. Julie's small flat was close enough to the Museum that they could walk, but even with an umbrella, wellingtons and raincoats, she and Oliver turned up soaking wet each morning. Spending the first half hour of each day drying themselves off by the creaky old pipes in the staffroom did little to lift their spirits.

By Thursday, Oliver had had enough.

"I wish Granny was still here," he sighed, pawing over the objects on the sensory table listlessly. "Then I could've stayed with her while you were at work."

Julie looked up from the new collection of fossils she

was arranging in one of the natural history room's glass cases. She wondered for a moment if she'd heard him correctly. In the past he'd sometimes mentioned wishing he could visit his father in Australia, even though he'd had no contact with him and they'd never even spoken on the phone. That unfulfilled yearning she could understand. But how could he possibly be missing his grandmother?

After years of estrangement, she'd taken Oliver to meet her mother a few times over the past couple of years. They'd met in neutral places – coffee shops and soft play centres where Oliver could run free, away from his grandmother's critical comments. It had always ended badly, with her mother blaming Julie for mollycoddling her son and turning him into another neurotic little copy of herself. He was never going to amount to anything either, her mother insinuated.

Not that she'd said any of that within Oliver's hearing. She did try to play the affectionate grandmother to him. But Julie could see that her smiles were tight-lipped and her words of praise were dripping with insincerity. Oliver was a smart boy. If her mother hadn't died last summer, it wouldn't have taken him long to work that out for himself. Maybe it had all been for the best.

"Your granny wouldn't have let you stay for the week," Julie said, running a hand across her tired eyes.

"She was always too busy for visitors."

"She wasn't too busy for *me*," Oliver said peevishly, building a small tower with the fossils. Julie didn't want to antagonise him further by telling him to take it down, so she just watched, reminding herself they were only plaster models and she could make more if necessary. "Granny liked me. She said I was a clever boy. She bought me nice presents."

She said you were cleverer than she expected, given that neither of your parents had amounted to much, Julie thought to herself angrily. *And she only bought you expensive gifts to shame me because I don't earn enough to buy you all the things you'd like.*

"Once the rain stops, we can get some nice flowers and put them in the cemetery for her, would you like that?" Julie asked, remembering her therapist's advice not to let her own relationship with her mother colour Oliver's memories of her.

"I guess," Oliver shrugged, looking uncertain. "She wants us to visit her. She's sad all on her own. She doesn't want to be by herself anymore." He turned his back on her and continued to play with the fossils and shells, making it clear he didn't want to talk about it further.

Julie frowned, trying to work out what he meant.

It must be something that's come up in therapy, she decided. *Maybe thinking about her in the present tense is a coping mechanism he's been taught. I'll need to talk to his therapist about it. I'm not sure I like that technique. Oliver's too sensitive for something like that.*

Julie sighed and continued her work, wishing she'd never agreed to that holiday with her mother. She'd been so close to Oliver before. The accident had opened up a gulf between them, and the expensive therapy didn't seem to be doing much to bridge it.

Maybe he's just too much like me, Julie thought, glancing over and seeing him putting the shells to his ears without the enthusiasm he used to have when he'd been building up his own collection. *He overthinks things and bottles everything up. Maybe my mother and her extroversion might have been a positive influence after all.*

"I'm just going to get another set of labels from the store cupboard," she told Oliver. "Don't wander off."

Looking over her shoulder as she left the room, she saw he was absorbed in his own examination of the shells. She was glad he'd found something to occupy himself with at last.

He's such a good boy, she thought as she headed to the general store at the back of the ground floor gallery. *Any of those other kids from the school groups we've had in this year would've been running wild by now and causing havoc. Everyone's been saying how well-behaved Oliver's been this week.*

She couldn't help feeling a small glow of pride that went some way to chasing away the gloom that had hung in a heavy cloud over the Museum ever since the terrible accident down in the toilets.

6.

When Julie got back to the natural history room, Oliver had gone.

She checked all of the gallery spaces on the ground floor and first floor, but he wasn't in any of them. By the time she'd been round the shop and offices on the lower ground floor, she'd started to panic.

"Don't worry, love, he won't have got far," Betty said, setting down the cup of tea she'd just poured herself in the staffroom. "Me and Jim will do another circuit of the Museum. You'll have missed him going round the place by yourself. And he is a growing boy – he can't be expected to sit on his bum every day for a whole week."

Feeling slightly reassured, Julie hurried out, checking the café again and making sure he wasn't in the paid exhibit area before heading back to the natural history room to see if he'd returned in her absence. At least he hadn't been in the toilets. After the horrible accident the other week, that was the first place she'd ruled out.

The natural history room was just as she'd left it, the case of new fossils standing open, waiting for her to finish labelling them. She closed it quickly before anyone noticed she'd left it unlocked. She'd been allowed to bring Oliver into work on the understanding that it wouldn't interfere with her tasks, and if the Director had caught her leaving valuable exhibits open to the public, she would have had some explaining to do.

Unsure where else to look, Julie turned to the sensory table where she'd last seen Oliver. The flat fossils were still stacked in a pile, and she quickly put them back in place, wondering if she should do another round of the galleries again, or leave it to Betty and Jim. She'd just made up her mind to head downstairs again and start another sweep of the whole building, when something strange made her pause.

There was something missing from the table.

She stared long and hard at the collection of shells and fossils, trying to work out what it was. The plaster ammonite, trilobite and gastropod casts were all still there, and Oliver had arranged the scallop and cowrie shells on the table in the shape of smiley faces. Distracted by her son's strange absence, it took Julie far longer than it should have done to recognise the obvious omission.

The large conch shell was gone.

As soon as she realised which shell was missing, Julie felt a knot of anxiety tighten in the pit of her stomach.

Why would he take that one out of this room? she wondered. *He knows he's not allowed to move any of the exhibits.*

She had a horrible feeling she knew the answer to that question.

The rain pounded on the window with renewed force as a fresh gust of wind drove it against the side of the building. Without knowing why, Julie found herself being drawn to the window where water was streaming like a torrent of tears.

She looked out, straining through the blur of rain to gaze across the park. Buses and cars were crawling down the road, their tyres churning up the flood water. She could barely see the railings of the bridge above the river, but even from this distance she could hear the roar of water rushing underneath, its currents swollen to breaking point by the non-stop rain.

There was a line of trees at the edge of the Museum carpark, and through them, Julie could just make out a small figure making slow progress across the boggy grass.

A shiver of horror ran down her spine.

It was Oliver. He was heading for the river, the conch

shell pressed to his ear.

Julie dropped the cabinet key she'd been holding and raced for the exit.

"Hey, Julie! Where are you—"

Julie charged past the front desk without stopping, the hem of her skirt getting stuck in the revolving doors when she pushed them too hard. Barely hearing the tearing of fabric, Julie rushed out into the rain, her blouse soaked through before she'd even made it across the carpark. The small figure she'd seen through the trees had disappeared, and she turned in circles on the grass, trying to work out which direction he might have taken.

Had Oliver crossed the bridge and headed up the road?

Would he have walked deeper into the park, perhaps to the old bandstand or the picnic benches?

Or…

Julie shivered, her whole body shaking as she realised where he'd gone and what it meant.

Running on, she came to the banks of the rushing river.

The water churned and frothed, overflowing onto the grass and pulling clods of earth into the current where they formed a witch's brew of white and brown. Julie scanned the river, her heart pounding.

He surely wouldn't…

PLEASE say he hasn't...

He had. In a muddy hollow, Julie could see several objects lying just out of reach of the foaming river. In a few more minutes, the rising water would carry them off too, never to be seen again.

Julie scrambled down the bank, moaning in horror. She knew what they meant even before she picked them up. One was the conch shell she'd seen Oliver pressing to his ear as he walked across the grass. The other was one of his shoes, which had got stuck in the bank when he'd...

Julie crumpled to her knees, her whole world collapsing around her.

Children's voices echoed in her head, a chorus of memories she wished she'd paid more attention to. The warning had been there, right from the start. If only she'd listened.

"She said she was cold," Ruby had whispered. *"She said I should get in the bath so we could be together."*

"Billy says I need to come and be with him," Jayden had told her. *"He says he's lonely."*

And then Oliver's voice, confused and troubled. *"She wants us to visit her. She's sad all on her own. She doesn't want to be by herself anymore."*

"Oliver..." Julie whispered, her heart almost bursting with pain. "My beautiful little boy..."

Her hands trembling, she lifted the conch shell and

held it to her ear.

At first, she could hear nothing over the roar of the river that lapped at her skirt as she knelt in the mud. And then the sound changed, no longer coming from outside, but from *inside* the shell. It wasn't just air that was trapped in the shell. It was a million voices of the drowned, their souls connected by the endlessly repeating water cycle.

"Mummy?" Julie heard Oliver's voice calling above the hiss of the current. "Mummy, where are you? It's cold and dark here. Mummy, I need you. Please come and get me. Mummy?"

"I'm coming, darling," Julie sobbed.

Dropping the conch shell in the mud, she took a last breath, and flung herself into the raging river.

Shielding their faces with umbrellas, the passers-by on the bridge above didn't notice the billowing skirt and tangled hair as a body was carried away on the current far below. They did notice, however, that the rain soon dried to a trickle, the river running calm once more. Had anyone stopped to pick up the conch shell lying on the bank, all they would have heard in its hidden depths was the whisper of waves on the wind and the timeless memory of water as a distant roaring died away to silence.

About the author

Victoria Williamson is an award-winning author from Glasgow, Scotland, who has worked as an educator in a number of different countries, including as an English teacher in China, a secondary school science teacher in Cameroon, a teacher trainer in Malawi, and an additional support needs teacher in the UK.

Her many visits to Kelvingrove Art Gallery and Museum from a young age inspired this set of short stories for adults based on the real and imaginary exhibits that captured her interest over the years, and led to her current studies of history and archaeology.

Victoria works part time writing books for the education company Twinkl and spends the rest of her time writing novels for children and adults, and visiting schools, libraries and literary festivals to give author talks and run creative writing workshops. When not writing or talking about books, she's often to be found up to her knees in mud on an archaeological dig or tangled up in a ball of wool playing with a crochet hook.

www.strangelymagical.com

@strangelymagic

Victoria and family at Kelvingrove Art Gallery and Museum in 1983 © The author.

Printed in Great Britain
by Amazon

59374711R00128